THE WAITING ROOM

By

J.S. Peck

BEJEWELED PUBLISHING
LAS VEGAS, NEVADA

Bejeweled Publishing
6480 Annie Oakley Drive
Suite 513
Las Vegas, Nevada 89120

ISBN# 978-1-7368837-1-6
First Edition: June 21, 2022

COVER ART DESIGN: Kelly A. Martin
INTERNAL DESIGN: Jake Naylor

SOME READER REVIEWS

I loved reading this book. The author is a master storyteller. I couldn't wait to keep reading. The characters are full and believable. I will anxiously await another book from this beloved author. [Bookbub]

♥ ♥ ♥

Wow, a great read. Three women who meet in the most common place and at a time when they all needed each other become true friends. These women form a long-lasting friendship that shares the highs and lows, marriages, children, and even murder. And bonds that last through the years. The twists and turns keep you turning every page. I love love loved it! Every woman should read this. Get one for each of your friends! [Goodreads]

♥ ♥ ♥

A very well-written book, it has some of the most expressive and vivid descriptions you'll ever read. [Goodreads]

♥ ♥ ♥

Wow. This book kept me on the edge of my seat throughout. Highly recommended. [Goodreads]

♥ ♥ ♥

This story was one terrific read with great character and plot development that kept me totally glued to my kindle until the turn of the very last page! I look forward to reading more from this author! [Goodreads]

♥ ♥ ♥

The writing was impeccable. It was easy to follow and get into. The characters were well developed with clear flaws that make them relatable and realistic, which is the mark of good character development. [Goodreads]

♥ ♥ ♥

The story is fast-paced and full of plot twists. Every time I thought I had the book all figured out, something would throw a curveball in my thought process. I found myself so frustrated at times, but that's a good thing when reading a book for me. I really enjoyed the writing style in this book as well. [Goodreads]

♥ ♥ ♥

I received an ARC copy of this book from the author - and put my marathon binge-watching of "Grace and Frankie" on hold. It's been a while since I've curled up in my chair and spent an entire day just reading - years probably - but I thoroughly enjoyed diving into this book of women and friendship and not climbing out to reality until the end. What an adventure of three women who meet by chance and have the chance to become great friends. Life needs more of this. As not-by-blood sisters, this book opens a portal that it is possible to support one another in this difficult world. I highly recommend adding this book to your e-reader or book pile. [Goodreads]

♥ ♥ ♥

...This would be an interesting book club pick! [Bookbub]

♥ ♥ ♥

...It was fun, even through the sad times, to spend time with these ladies and watch how their lives blossom and change. I want to thank the author for allowing me to read an arc for an honest review. [Bookbub]

♥ ♥ ♥

This is a delightful book about three women who meet in the waiting room of a doctor's office. They talk together while they wait. Shortly after their meeting, they decide to meet for coffee. This is just the beginning of a wonderful friendship for them. Soon they become very close friends and really come to depend on each other. The characters in this book are real and show how good friends can change your life. There are several problems that arise, and every time they help each other through their difficulties. It gives you a good feeling that you can have people you can depend on. I received an ARC of this book, and this is my honest review. [Bookbub]

DEDICATION

Here's to you, girlfriends! I dedicate this book to GIRLFRIENDS everywhere! Girlfriends of all ages enrich each other's lives and all those around them with their loving, fun, all-knowing spirits. We women have the power to change the world into a more forgiving place by treating others with the same kindness and love we give our besties.

TABLE OF CONTENTS

1983
Chapter 1
Allison

Trying not to panic, the three women sat in the small cubby area designated for those who hadn't cleared their examination. Their striped oversized wraparound gowns did nothing for their appearance, making them as self-conscious as if they were stripped naked and wore nothing at all.

At least, that was how Allison felt as she tried to avoid the other two women studiously doing the same. Each of them sat in their self-made bubble of privacy, caught up in concern and what-ifs. Curiosity got the better of her, and Allison found herself focusing on the other women, taking them in. The women ignored her, remaining within their thoughts, and Allison turned away to give them privacy. She found it took greater effort to ignore them, yet, determined to do just that, Allison picked up a worn magazine from the empty chair next to her and began to thumb through the pages. Finally, she couldn't stand it any longer and exclaimed, "This is cheery, isn't it? My name is Allison Sullivan, by the way."

At first, the two women appeared startled at being addressed, her words sounding deafening as they broke the silence. But then, they relaxed enough to smile and indulge her by offering up their names. "Hi, my name is Bella Jones," said the pretty woman looking to be in her 30s with coffee-colored skin and a wide smile. With her sparkling dark eyes, there was a playfulness about her that was pleasing.

After hesitating, the other woman stated primly, "I'm Marianne Houghton." It was easy to see she was the tallest of the three with long blond hair, knotted severely at the back of her neck, and blue eyes that appeared slightly haunted. She seemed guarded and looked about the same age as the other two but appeared the most worried.

Any further conversation was interrupted when two nurses stepped into the room. One leaned over Marianne and spoke in a soft voice. "You can get dressed now, Marianne, and leave, but you'll need to be rechecked in six months. It's late in the day, and the front office is closed, so you'll need to call us tomorrow to set up your appointment."

The nurse patted Marianne's shoulder in support before turning away and leaving. Marianne looked dazed but gamely stood and headed into the curtained locker area to change.

The second nurse stood in front of Bella. "Congratulations. You're all clear. We'll see you next year."

Bella smiled. "Thanks."

Then the nurse at Bella's side turned. "Allison?" she asked, looking at her notes. "Good news for you too. Make sure you make your appointment for next year, okay?"

Allison stood and checked her clothes out of the locker that was temporarily hers and went behind her own curtained area to get dressed. The three women finished dressing and emptied from their private dressing rooms, relieved. They left the doctor's office in a group and stood together, waiting for the elevator to arrive.

It was dusk outside, and the stress of the day began to collapse, and their moods lightened. Then, Allison looked at the other two and asked on the spur of the moment, "Ladies, are you up for a glass of wine at the cocktail lounge downstairs? My treat."

"After this day? Heck, yeah!" answered Bella with a wicked grin.

They both looked to Marianne. "Why not?" she replied, seeming to perk up at the thought. However, a bit of sadness surrounded her that was hard to identify yet remained.

As they unloaded off the elevator, Allison impulsively hooked her arms through the arms of the other two, and the three of them entered the pub area light-hearted and laughing. The bartender looked up at them and smiled. "Ah, ladies, in for a night of fun?"

They laughed and headed for the larger booth in the back. The waitress followed them there and asked, "What can I get you, ladies? Cosmos are our special for tonight. Interested?"

They nodded, and she turned to holler at the bartender, "Three specials, Mike! Is there anything else I can get you?" she asked.

"Not right now," Marianne was quick to answer.

The waitress left and returned within minutes, placing their drinks in front of them. "Enjoy!" she said before she turned and left.

Allison hoisted her glass and knocked it against the others being held up. "Here's to us … none better," she toasted.

Bella and Marianne laughed, and then Bella said, "Amen." She grinned and said, "Let me spell that out for you so that you don't think I said, 'Ah, men.'"

They chuckled. Allison said, "That wouldn't work for me today, either, sister."

"What a day," groaned Bella as she leaned against the back of the booth. "My boyfriend wanted to know what it was like to have a mammogram," she laughed.

"What did you tell him?" Allison asked.

"I told him, 'Think of going into the garage, lying down on your side on the hard cement floor, then, picture the car backing over your boobs,'" she chuckled, covering her mouth with her hand.

Hearing that, Marianne spit out some of her drink, trying to hold in her laughter. She covered her chest with her hands, leaned forward, swallowed, and then began to laugh uncontrollably. They all joined in until each of them was wiping her eyes. "Oh, my God! I haven't laughed like that in a long time," admitted Marianne.

Having laughed so hard, Marianne looked like a completely different person—vibrant and stunningly beautiful.

The waitress headed over to them. "Another round, ladies?"

They looked at each other and immediately nodded. Then, the waitress headed off, and the girls sat back and relaxed. They were having fun, and nothing was going to interfere with their time together.

One by one, they released the stress of the day even more. "What do you do for work, Bella?" asked Allison.

"I'm a doctor at Children's Hospital specializing in children with cancer."

"Wow! That's a trip," Allison said, impressed. "I think that would be difficult to do, knowing the odds aren't that great for recovery."

"You get used to it because the kids who aren't going to make it intuitively know they won't and usually handle it much better than the parents do. They are amazing kids," she solemnly explained.

"What about you, Marianne? What is it that you do?" Allison asked.

"I'm a paralegal working at the Benson & Sons law firm."

"That's cool," Allison said. "The one in the financial district? How long have you been with them?"

"Ever since I moved to Boston five years ago, actually," Marianne replied. "It's okay," she said without much enthusiasm.

"What about you, Allison? What do you do?" asked Bella.

"Right now, I'm between jobs. I'm interviewing for a position at the First National Bank downtown," she answered. "In their loan department."

"That sounds like a pretty important job," Marianne said. "Have you always been in finance?"

"God, no! I'm not even sure I'll be able to sit behind a desk all day, but I thought I might as well give it a shot," she laughed.

As the evening wore on and they were nearly finished with their drinks, Marianne started to check her watch every few minutes. "What's up, Marianne?" asked Bella.

"Sorry to say, I've got to get home. My dog needs to be let out and fed."

"What kind of dog do you have?" Allison asked.

Marianne's face lit up. "She's a miniature black poodle. Her name is Sophie."

"She sounds cute," Bella said.

"She is," agreed Marianne, smiling.

"I should be going, too," Bella said, looking at her watch.

"Before you leave, are you two game to meet up again?" Allison asked. "Here, next week? Same time?"

Bella and Marianne smiled and nodded.

"Why not?" Bella added. "I have the next day off."

They exchanged contact information, hugged, and left, each sensing their unusual relationship was worth the effort and they might end up as friends for life, always answering the question of how they met with—*the waiting room.*

Chapter 2
Allison

As Allison marched along the streets of Boston, heading toward the North End, where she lived, her heart was happy. Meeting Bella and Marianne was a blessing, she thought, particularly at a time in her life where she felt utterly alone after being unceremoniously dumped by the man she'd been dating. Even though she knew that he was unsuitable in so many ways, and it was best for her to no longer be involved with him, it still hurt to have it end.

She thought of her new friends. Bella seemed so grounded, so sure of herself despite being black in a white man's world. And who has a job like hers except for saints or angels? On top of that, she was quick to laugh at simple things that had been said. Yes, it would be wonderful to count Bella as a friend.

Marianne was an enigma to her. She spoke with a slight southern accent and was prim like most people from the south were. Yet, Allison felt there was a wild side to Marianne that she kept stuffed inside. It would be interesting to see how their relationship developed, and she was excited to see how that might work out.

As Allison crossed under the viaduct and walked into the North End (the Italian part of Boston), she was met with tantalizing odors of olive oil, garlic, and spices in significant contrast to the smells of the garbage set out on the street waiting to be picked up.

"Allison! Wait up!" Susan, her roommate, called out.

"Hi! Where did you come from?" asked Allison, surprised.

Susan laughed. "You walked right past me. You were talking to yourself and not paying attention to anything around you."

"Sorry about that. How goes it?" Allison asked, eying the slim, dark-haired beauty.

"Good. Matt and I just met for a drink. I was hoping he wanted to do more than having a drink, though," she said wistfully.

"I'm sure that you can make that happen soon enough," Allison stated bluntly while knocking into her playfully.

Susan was model beautiful and used her beauty to dangerously pull men into her bed, much like a spider catching a fly into her web. Allison had seen it happen enough times, thinking of all the occurrences when she'd had to listen to the noises coming from the next bedroom in the apartment they shared. Whether Allison liked it or not, thanks to the old, thin walls, she had been in the background of some of Susan's intimate moments despite her not wanting to be included. A good noise-canceling headset helped but didn't always do the trick.

Susan's behavior caused Allison to be on guard during those times that Susan's careless indifference toward her date caused him to become angry at her lack of feeling toward him. If Susan wasn't careful, one of her dates' outbursts was going to be more than simple shouting, demanding more from her. At the thought, Allison shivered as a cold wind blew across her shoulders.

Allison and Susan walked side by side down the middle of the narrow street with old brick apartment buildings towering over them on each side, heading to their apartment. It was a warm, balmy night with a gentle breeze blowing. Allison was grateful that she lived in such an exciting place. Living with all the Italian families was a unique experience because those in the North End seemed to be stuck in time with the older women dressed in black, spending countless hours at church praying for their family and God knows what else.

Suddenly, Susan stopped and pulled on Allison's arm as they stood under a street light. "Hey, let me see!" she urged, turning her toward the light. "You've got blue in your hair!" she exclaimed.

Allison blushed. "Yeah, I got it done this morning. I needed to do something to perk myself up. So, you like it?"

"I do," Susan answered. "It's so cool! I'm glad to see you coming out of your funk," she added sincerely.

Allison smiled tightly. "It's always the little things that make a difference, isn't it?"

"Damn straight." Susan's brow wrinkled. "Isn't it a little late for you to be out? Not normal for you. What have you been up to?"

"I had my mammogram this afternoon, and afterward, I met up with two ladies from there to have a drink."

"Really? Anyone I might know?"

"I doubt it."

"Where did you meet them?" she questioned.

"In the waiting room," Allison answered. "At the doctor's office."

"Leave it to you, roomie," Susan said before she entered the apartment building where Allison stood, holding the door open, waiting for her to enter.

Allison smiled to herself. Susan hated anything to do with doctors or their offices. Since she had met the girls at one, maybe that'd be enough for Susan not to compete with Allison right away for the attention of her new friends.

Susan craved to be the center of attention. Her neediness often caused her to push her way into any conversation Allison was having, leaving Allison on the sidelines, quietly watching Susan take over. Allison let her get away with it most times, figuring it was not worth the hassle of an argument that she couldn't win. As many times as Allison tried to explain it to her, Susan never grasped why Allison could be upset with her. What was that expression? You can lead a horse to water, but you can't make him drink."

If it ever mattered enough to her, Allison would fight for it. So far, not too much had. Life was too short to sweat the small things.

Chapter 3
Bella

Bella entered the Park Street station and waited on the platform for the orange line train that would take her to the stop in Roxbury where she lived. Instead of being one of the poorer sections of Boston as it was known, Roxbury and the Mission Hills area was just beginning to be renovated and would someday, undoubtedly, be considered a fashionable, trendy place to live. Thanks to being the only grandchild, Bella was the proud owner of the small two-bedroom townhouse there that her grandmother had left her in her will. During all those strenuous years of her residency as a doctor at Brigham and Women's Faulkner Hospital in Boston, having that place to live nearby had saved her life, or, more to the point, saved her pocketbook.

Bella was grateful to her grandmother every time she stepped through the door of her place.

As she neared her townhouse, she saw her neighbor's child riding his "big wheel" up and down the sidewalk in front of their building. Bella stooped down to speak to the little three-year-old boy when she got closer. "Hi there, Samuel! Are you having fun?"

Samuel looked at her with a grin. "Look at me! See how fast I can go!" he hollered over his shoulder as he began to pump his little legs as fast as he could.

She called out to him. "Wow! You sure are speedy, Samuel!" She smiled and nodded at the older woman, watching over him … his babysitter, most likely.

Then she climbed the stairs and entered her home. Despite the enjoyable break of spending time with the new women in her life, Bella was tired. When she opened the front door and walked into the living room, she pulled in a deep breath and tried not to be annoyed at seeing the newspaper thrown carelessly onto the floor, spreading out like spilled milk. Empty food wrappers were left on the coffee table, along with a half-eaten carton of Chinese food. Was this what she could expect living with someone who didn't think being tidy was necessary?

She grabbed the empty wrappers, leaving the carton behind, and walked into the kitchen. There, on the table, was a scribbled note from Benjamin. "Gone out. Be back later. P.S. I left you some Chinese food."

She peeked into the refrigerator and saw that it was nearly empty with no cartons of Chinese food inside.

She walked back into the living room and peered into the almost empty carton of Chow Mein, and grunted. So that was his idea of leaving her dinner? It was a good thing she'd stopped and bought a few groceries on her way home.

Thinking that living together would give them more time to grow their relationship, Bella had allowed Benjamin to move in with her several months ago. However, the more she thought about Benjamin's note, the clearer it became that their relationship was anything but right for either of them. They hardly connected or saw each other because of their jobs—she a doctor, he a lawyer. When they did see each other, they fought, frustrated at not being given the necessary attention to keep a healthy relationship growing. The question now became, what was she going to do about it?

She looked at the leftover Chinese food and lost her appetite. She dumped it into the garbage and pulled out an apple to munch on as she put away her groceries. She washed the dirty dishes and straightened up the kitchen before she readied herself for bed.

Tossing the covers over her nude body, she closed her eyes and fell into a deep sleep. Later, she came out of a dreamless fog to feel Benjamin's hand clutching her breasts before trailing down toward her center. She was irritated that he would do such a thing without her being awake enough to agree to what he was doing. "Benjamin! Stop!"

"What's the matter, baby? You like when I do this," he murmured in a husky voice, laced with need.

"I do if I'm awake enough to be part of it," she protested.

"C'mon, baby, don't be like that," he implored, his words shaded with annoyance.

She was exhausted and surrendered to his needs. Their lovemaking, without the joy of foreplay, turned into something for them just to get through. After doing the "deed," Benjamin fell into a deep sleep, resting on his back, snoring with an opened mouth. The alcoholic odor on his breath tainted the air around him.

Bella, now awake, leaned on her elbow and stared at him, wondering once more what she was going to do about their deteriorating relationship. How important was it to her, anyhow? They seemed to be out of sync in more ways than their time schedules.

She sighed, knowing the truth. The most satisfying thing in her life right now was all the children who, upon sight, grabbed her heart—the children with cancer—the children who were braver than she could ever be. Before now, she had not known what it meant when she heard the term "old soul." For the children to go through what they endured fighting cancer, they had to have lived many lifetimes to have the peace of knowing they'd soon be "home" where there was unconditional love. At first, she'd found that idea hard to believe, but many of the children in her care had explained just that to her after seeing her worried brow. Just thinking of them brought tears to her eyes.

She wiped away the wetness on her face and vowed to make the necessary changes in her relationship. She thought back to the women she'd had drinks with and wondered what they would do in her situation. She had liked them because they were so different from her in ways more than the color of their skin. There was something special about the three of them being together. She was sure they'd become close friends. She felt it in her bones.

She smiled, thinking of them. Allison was a free spirit. She had liked her right away, the blue in her hair giving her a defiant flair that Bella admired. She was relaxed and easy to be with without any expectations, and Allison didn't treat her differently because of her color. That would be a deal-breaker. She didn't want anyone to act unnatural or fuss over her because she was black.

Bella frowned, thinking it might take Marianne a bit of time before reaching that state of indifference. Marianne seemed more proper with her slight southern accent and would probably be the sane one of the three, applying brakes when she thought things were a little too lax. Yet, there was something about Marianne Bella liked despite her seeming sadness and standoffish persona. When she'd come out of her shell to laugh at Bella's description of having a mammogram, it had shown her what a different person Marianne was when she smiled.

♥ ♥ ♥

After Benjamin left for work, the phone rang, breaking into Bella's thoughts. A quick look at her cell phone showed her father's face, making her groan. She loved her father; she really did. But he'd made his bed as far as she was concerned when he'd married someone nearly 20 years younger. It was hard for her father to adjust to his new life with a squalling baby added to the mix, even though the baby was adorable. She had heard more from her father since the baby's birth than ever before. She thought that it was her father's way of escaping for a few minutes from all that was happening at home.

"Hi, Dad, what's up?"

"Hi, kiddo. I was wondering if you're available to babysit Jonathan for a few hours while I take your mother out to dinner tonight."

"Dad," she scolded. "Priscilla is not my mother, and you know it."

"I just wish the two of you could get along," he lamented with a sigh.

"Stop trying to make that happen, okay, Dad? I'll acknowledge that she's legally my stepmother, but no one anywhere can take the place of Mom. If she were alive, she'd set you straight, right?"

Her father chuckled. "She sure would, honey."

"Dad? About tonight—no can do. I'm on call at the hospital. Maybe Aunt Mary will be available."

"Okay, I'll phone her. Is everything all right with you?"

"All is fine, Dad. I'll talk to you later, okay? I love you."

"Love you, too, Baby Girl."

After ending the call, Bella's eyes filled. Lord, she missed her mother every day. Watching her suffer from cancer had pushed Bella to excel to the top of her class to become the excellent medical oncologist she was today.

She looked at her watch and realized that she'd need to hurry to make it to the hospital in time for her shift.

Chapter 4
Marianne

After saying good night to Allison and Bella, Marianne decided not to call for a cab as she usually would have. Since the weather was so pleasant, she felt safe enough to walk to her house instead. For the slight difference in time that it would take her, Sophie would be okay until Marianne arrived home to let her outside.

Halfway there, Marianne picked up her pace as she parted her way through the downtown crowds of people out in force on such a lovely evening. Newbury Street was popular, and the stores, pubs, and cafes were trendy—a place where people gathered, particularly on a Friday night. As she neared home, she felt proud to be one of the lucky ones able to afford to live in one of the beautiful upscale townhouses that stood on the small hill within the city limits.

Beacon Hill was a beautiful, protected, historic section of Boston, home to the Massachusetts State House and other historical landmarks. It included the Boston African American National Historic Site, which interpreted 15 pre-Civil War structures relating to the history of Boston's 19th century African-American community. Beacon Hill was one of the oldest communities and received its name from the beacon that once stood high on the hill to warn locals about invasions.

Bypassing the African Meeting House as she did many days, Marianne's thoughts turned to the two women she'd met at the doctor's office. She enjoyed spending time with Allison and Bella and was aware that she probably appeared stiff in front of them. But the truth was as much as Marianne lived in an area once defined as African-American, she didn't have much experience being around black people socially. Her strict Aunt Eveline had made sure of that.

After her parents had died in a car accident, Marianne was sent to live with her father's only sibling in Atlanta, Georgia, at seven years old. Her widowed and very proper aunt treated her responsibility of raising Marianne like a heavy burden that didn't allow any opportunity to begin life anew with another man. Therefore, Marianne felt she was somehow to blame for any unhappiness that showed on her aunt's face. Sensitive to that, Marianne was unsure of her aunt's love for her. It was only after she'd inherited all of her aunt's many assets that she began to understand that she must have loved her when her will referred to her as "my beautiful niece, Marianne, who has brought me so much happiness."

Even though her life hadn't been unhappy, and she and her aunt had shared some enjoyable times, sadness still clung to Marianne to think she'd let all those years pass between them without making more of an effort to let her aunt know how much she was grateful to have been brought up by her. Marianne had come to realize that she and her aunt were very much alike in that she'd pushed her aunt away as much as had been the reverse—two women unable to easily express their true feelings for each other.

After Marianne had moved into her townhouse, she took daily walks to the Boston Commons, America's oldest city public park in the United States (dating from 1634), close to her house. There, she observed others having a love affair with their pets, and she thought about getting a dog of her own. And dogs at the park seemed to like her, especially one miniature poodle named Sophie. One day, the dog's owner explained to Marianne that she was moving and wasn't allowed to have a dog and asked her if she'd be interested in taking Sophie. Marianne immediately agreed. The dog had been with her for the past two years, and Marianne considered adopting Sophie as one of the best decisions she'd made in her life.

Marianne climbed the stairs to her house and, as soon as she hit the landing, she heard Sophie barking on the other side of the door. It amazed her how the dog knew she was outside and always waited eagerly to greet her. It warmed her heart. As soon as she opened the door and stepped in, Marianne sighed with pleasure at seeing the coziness she had created with her discerning taste in choosing the right pieces that worked well together. She had a flair for it.

She bent and scooped up the dog into her arms. As soon as she did, Sophie began licking her face with such intent that it made Marianne giggle like a young girl unable to hold back her joy. She walked down the hallway toward the back of the house, where she slid the glass door open and stepped outside, setting the dog down gently onto the brick patio. Sophie took off like a shot and ran to the far corner of the small yard to do her thing. Marianne smiled with contentment when she watched Sophie race back to her. However, when she heard her house phone ring, her smile faded. Marianne was pretty sure she knew who was calling—Jeremy Loveland III—the man she was "supposed to" marry.

Her purported fiancé was someone her aunt had pushed onto her before she died. He was the grandson of one of her aunt's few close friends and came from an established family in Georgia—a family who in modern times had lost their "old money" and now had to find their way in life like most people unless they married into money.

So far, despite Jeremy's purported striking good looks, she was not eager to get married—to anyone at this time.

Marianne let the phone ring, not playing into Jeremy's games of pressuring her to go out with him. Believing he was only attracted to her money, she had no interest in him at all. She picked up Sophie and went inside.

Chapter 5
One Week Later

Allison wasn't surprised to find that she was the first to arrive at the pub. She was always early and, as her mother had pointed out many times, "You were always a curious child, never wanting to miss out on anything."

The same waitress as last week approached her with a smile. "Back again, I see. Are the other two ladies going to be joining you?"

"Yes, we're back for more Cosmos. Can we sit in the same booth as before?"

"Sure, why not. Let me check and make sure it's cleared off."

Through the window, Allison saw Marianne rushing toward the front entrance. A few minutes later, she ran into the pub in a flurry and immediately apologized when she saw Allison standing there. "I'm so sorry to be late."

"You're right on time, actually," Allison responded with a smile, noting the hands on the wall clock. "The waitress is getting our booth ready."

"Wonderful," Marianne said. "Is Bella coming?"

"Yup, she texted that she'd be a few minutes late, though."

The waitress waved them over and then stood by the table while they scooted into the booth. "Ready for your Cosmos, ladies?"

"We're going to wait for Bella. She should be here any minute now," Allison said.

Settling in and wanting to break the stiffness of their new relationship, Allison asked Marianne, "How's Sophie?"

Marianne relaxed and smiled broadly. "I can't wait for you and Bella to meet her. She's such a cutie."

Just then, Bella came bouncing up to the table. "I'm so glad I could make it in time. How are you, ladies?" she asked as she slid into the booth. "Did you have a good week?"

Both women answered with raised shoulders and a tilt of the head, indicating it was so-so. "How about you?" Allison asked.

Bella rolled her eyes. "Can we order our drinks first?" she answered as she waved the waitress over.

"Ready for the Cosmos?" the waitress asked.

They all nodded, and she left them. Bella leaned back against the booth and closed her eyes, and didn't say anything until after the waitress set their drinks down before them. Then, she opened her eyes and looked between them. "It's been a long week for me. I could use your advice."

Marianne cocked her head, perking up. Working at a law office had taught her to listen carefully to whatever was said. Yet, very few people ever asked her for her opinion.

Allison had always been a good listener and studied Bella, trying to read her energy. "Sure. What's up?"

Bella flushed, looking embarrassed before drawing in a big breath. "I allowed my boyfriend to move in with me, and now I can't get him to leave. Any advice?"

"Is the relationship over?" asked Marianne in a solemn voice.

"I've been trying to tell him that, but he says he loves me. Besides, I don't think he has any other place to go."

"Why is that your problem?" Allison asked.

"He can't afford to live on his own?" Marianne added.

Bella flushed. "He makes good enough money working at the largest law firm downtown, so I'm sure he can."

"But you're torn about wanting him to go, right?" asked Allison.

Bella grimaced, caught in the truth. "To be honest, I don't have a lot of experience dating men. I've always been so driven to become a doctor that I never allowed any romantic liaisons to develop. However, Benjamin is such a charmer that I let him into my life. He's a good man, but we're on such different time schedules that we're like two ships passing in the night."

"How's the sex?" asked Allison bluntly.

Bella reddened. "Pretty nice, actually."

"So, that's what you'll miss then. I get it. A good sex partner can make things seem okay, but you need to make sure other things are good as well. I got caught up in a relationship like that ... it was such a mess," Allison lamented.

Marianne listened to the two of them talk about sex partners and blushed. She wasn't used to anyone sharing anything that intimate with her. She'd had a boyfriend at college, and they'd had intercourse twice, and as far as she was concerned, it was nothing to write home about. She was jolted out of her reverie when Allison asked, "Any ideas, Marianne?"

"I haven't had much experience dating either, but working on some of the cases at my law firm, I think you need to nip this in the bud before it gets out of hand," Marianne answered.

Bella and Allison nodded in agreement. Then Allison began to bop up and down in her seat and click her fingers as she sang, "Hit the road, Jack, and don't ya come back no more, no more, no more ...."

The other two smiled and shook their heads at Allison's silliness.

Bella said. "What about you? Are you girls in a relationship?"

A flash of sadness crossed Allison's brow. "Was. I really liked this guy and thought it was going somewhere until I found out he was cheating on me. After he'd dumped me, I caught him trying to get my roommate to hook up with him." Sympathetic looks from Bella and Marianne made her add, "That's not anything new, though. Every man I've ever dated can't help but be intrigued by my roommate. You'll see."

"I'm so sorry, Allison," Bella said.

Allison shrugged her shoulders as if to say, "It is what it is."

Marianne said, "The guy sounds like a loser. I think you're better off without him."

"How about you, Marianne? Are you in a relationship?" asked Bella.

She looked uncertain for a moment. "I have someone who wants to get together with me, but I'm not interested," she answered, reddening. The girls eagerly leaned toward her, wanting the skinny about what was going on. Seeing that, Marianne hastily added, "It's a long story, not worth getting into," barring any further information. Since Marianne wasn't going to share more at this time, Bella and Allison leaned back in the booth.

"Well then, it looks like the three of us are footloose and fancy-free. There's a concert in Boston Common tomorrow if you want to go. Cyndi Lauper is performing for free, and I don't have to work," Bella said.

"Count me in," Allison proclaimed, grinning.

Bella looked to Marianne. "How about you?"

She was surprised to be invited because her usual reserve and unapproachable aura prevented others from asking her anywhere. "Sure, count me in too," Marianne beamed.

"Afterward, I want to hit Filene's Basement. They're having a fabulous sale. Anyone interested in joining me?" asked Allison.

Bella and Marianne nodded.

They laughed and talked about some of their "finds" from Filenes when Allison's roommate approached, surprising them. She beamed her winning smile and scanned the table. "Hi, I'm Susan Richards, Allison's roommate. You don't mind if I join you, do you?"

Allison's face grew pink with exasperation. "Don't you have a date?"

"Not until later. I was bored staying at home. I didn't think you'd mind if I had one drink with you all."

Marianne had already begun to slide over to make room for her in the semi-circular booth. Bella took one look at Allison's face and reached under the table for Allison's hand in support.

The tension in the air caused the conversation to come to a standstill, and Allison shifted in her seat, trying not to be annoyed. Marianne looked at her, questioning what was happening. Unaware, Susan took over the conversation, and Allison noticed how easily she had outmaneuvered her once more in competing for her friendships. And truthfully, it was difficult not to be entranced by Susan's exceptional beauty. Any woman who saw her unconsciously pulled in her stomach, stood taller, and checked her nail polish. Allison sighed. Knowing she couldn't change what was, she squeezed Bella's hand, determined to relax and join in the fun.

After several minutes of chatter and laughter, a good-looking man left the pub area and walked to their table. "It sounds like you're having too much fun. May I join you?" Then, confident of a positive response, he moved closer.

Susan immediately patted the seat next to her and pushed Marianne away to move further into the booth. Then, she got out and let the man slide in before her. Marianne looked across at Allison and rolled her eyes. Both Bella and Allison saw her do this and chuckled.

The man called the waitress over to the table and ordered a round of drinks on him. He exuded sex with his tanned skin over chiseled features, smoldering green eyes, brown hair pulled back in a small fashionable ponytail, and an aura of power and danger surrounding him. It was evident that he was used to getting his way as he leaned into Susan, drinking her in.

When the waitress came with the beverages, she had to tap him on the shoulder so he would move away from Susan enough to place his drink on the table. The man couldn't take his eyes off Susan or her large breasts. He was entranced with her … and Susan was aware of it. It didn't take too long for the three women to eye each other, uncomfortable as they watched their foreplay taking place with their words, touches, and innuendoes.

Finally, Allison snapped, "Get a room, for God's sake."

Susan had the decency to blush. Looking at her watch, she said, "It's time for me to go, anyway. Then, turning to Allison, she said, "Don't wait up for me."

"Go? You can't leave now!" the man protested angrily. As Susan stood up, he grabbed her arm. "You can't just walk away from me after what just took place!"

Susan pulled away from him. "I'm sure the girls won't mind if you stayed," she responded with a bored look and a dismissing pat on his shoulder. She waved her fingers at all of them before turning and walking to the door.

The man sat there, angry. He eyed the three who remained and quickly said, "I need to go, too," as he rose and hurried off.

Allison was sitting in a position to see him rushing toward the exit, trying to catch up with Susan. She sighed. Trouble loomed; she could feel it in her bones. Susan wasn't aware that her easy dismissal of her admirers didn't always sit well with them. She asked the other two, "Did you get his name?"

They shook their heads.

"I see what you mean about Susan," Bella said.

"Yup. It never fails. She's so used to getting all the attention that it never dawns on her that she might be intruding."

"She's gorgeous," Marianne said, pushing her hair behind her ear and holding her hand out to check her nails.

Allison noted her movements but said nothing. She was used to it.

The waitress came and handed the bill to Allison. When she scanned it, Allison groaned and shook her head in disbelief. "You're not going to believe this. The jerk never paid for our drinks."

"What?" Bella and Marianne said in one voice.

"No worries, I'll take care of it," Allison said.

"You will not!" proclaimed Marianne, ripping the bill from Allison's hand, knowing Allison was between jobs. When they both started to protest, she said, "I've got this, please."

As they parted ways, each headed in a different direction, they promised to meet the next day at the corner of Tremont and Summer Street for the concert. They had no idea it would be a day that would change their lives forever.

Chapter 6

Allison woke up to a strangely quiet apartment. Often, a male would wander around with a towel wrapped around him—or nothing at all—grabbing some coffee for himself and Susan.

Allison got up, pulled out the coffee beans from the freezer, and began the ritual of grinding them to make her favorite blend of coffee. She bought the coffee from a small shop in the North End that roasted their own coffee beans. The aroma was tantalizing as she took in deep breaths, inhaling the surrounding air with anticipation.

She shivered when a cool breeze passed over her, and Susan's face flashed before her. *I hope she's okay,* she thought and shivered again. Allison usually didn't worry about her roommate when she spent the night elsewhere. After all, Susan was an adult and could choose to do what she wanted. Still, Allison's unease grew.

Thinking of the evening before, Allison shook her head at Susan's boldness. What was that girl thinking? Despite Susan's annoying behavior of constantly butting in, Allison loved and cared about her. She knew that her roommate's neediness came from being raised in a strict household without much love. And she'd seen that for herself the times Allison had been with Susan's parents.

To get her mind off Susan, Allison turned on the radio and sat at the tiny kitchen table next to the window that looked over the street below. She grasped the coffee tight in her hands and swayed with the music. Promoting the upcoming concert, the radio station played a song by Cindi Lauper, and she became excited to meet her friends to see the singer in person. If Allison didn't want to be late, she'd have to hurry. First, she had to get to the laundromat, and then she needed to buy some groceries, especially more coffee beans. She ran for the shower, glad that she didn't have to wait her turn as she did most days when Susan took forever in the bathroom.

As she got out of the shower, she heard pounding at the door, becoming demanding enough not to be ignored. Allison grabbed a towel to wrap around her dripping body and ran to answer it. "Who is it?" she called through the locked, closed door.

"It's me, Matt."

"Susan's not here. Try her later; she should be back then."

"But ..." he began.

"I haven't got time now. I'll tell Susan you came by," Allison promised.

It amazed Allison how many of Susan's dates thought she had nothing better to do than play secretary and pass messages onto Susan. She grimaced. "I promise, Matt."

He left without thanking her, and Allison dashed back to the bathroom to fix her hair and apply makeup. She needed to stick to her schedule if she didn't want to be late to meet the girls.

♥ ♥ ♥

As Bella rolled over in bed, she heard Benjamin snoring. She grabbed her robe, made her way out into the tiny sitting area between the two bedrooms, and found him asleep on the small couch, feet hanging over the edge. He was still fully dressed and looked uncomfortable in his position, but he never stirred as she watched him. It was apparent he'd come in late and hadn't wanted to disturb her and crashed on the only available spot that was not her bed. As much as she was thankful to him for letting her get a good night's sleep, she knew it was time to remain strong and nip their relationship in the bud, as Marianne had said.

After she filled the kettle for tea, she rinsed out her favorite mug. Once the tea had steeped to her liking, she took it outside to sit on the patio. She smiled when she saw her neighbor's cat on the fence dividing the space between the neighbor's lawn and hers. The cat loved sitting there so he could eye the birds that flittered about the single apple tree in her yard and taunted him.

Bella leaned back in her chair and sipped the spicy tea, her thoughts on the previous evening. She found it amazing that she felt close to Allison and Marianne as if they were her long-time friends … especially since they were white. She didn't have any girlfriends of that color. From the little Bella knew about them, they'd have had no reason to experience what it was like to be black during a time of such racial discrimination. She wondered if her skin color would affect their relationship if there came a time when they found themselves on opposite sides of an argument because of it.

Lost in her thoughts, Bella smelled him before she felt his kiss on the top of her head … alcohol breath. When she looked up, Benjamin was already moving toward the other chair. "Morning," he mumbled in a hoarse voice.

"Good morning," she responded automatically.

He patted down his afro hair, cleared his throat, and then leaned toward her. "You're serious about wanting me to move out, then?"

"I think it's for the best, Benjamin, don't you? We never have time for each other, and that's not a good way to grow a healthy relationship. I don't want to end up resenting you."

"I agree," he replied, nodding.

Immediately Bella was on the alert. No arguing? What was with that? When she'd first brought it to his attention, he was adamant that he didn't want to break up. And now? "So, what's happened between last week and now, Benjamin, for you to change your mind."

His eyes didn't meet hers. "I ran into my old girlfriend."

"And?"

His face suffused with pleasure. "She wants me back."

Bella was aware that Benjamin hadn't been the one who'd wanted that relationship to end, so she understood why he was so pleased. Yet, she knew enough to realize that most of those reconnects didn't work out. "So, what did you decide to do?" Bella demanded.

"Well, I'm going to try it again with her. Like you said, our relationship isn't exactly working," he said, his hand motioning between himself and her.

Out of nowhere, a flash of anger filled her. "It sure didn't take you long to change your mind about us," she scorned.

"Why? Are you jealous?" he asked with raised brows.

"Of course not. I'm happy for you," she replied through gritted teeth, forcing herself to take the high road.

"Okay, then. I'll pack up and be out of your way. It shouldn't take too long." Not wanting their relationship to end in anger, he grabbed for her arm as she walked around his chair, but she was too upset to let him touch her and kept on moving. Yes, she knew it was best if he left, but it still hurt.

"Just leave the keys on the kitchen table and lock the door when you leave," she demanded as she hurriedly left to get ready to meet the girls. Thank God she had plans with them today because she wouldn't have been able to stay here and watch him pack up and leave without breaking down.

♥ ♥ ♥

Marianne was out of breath as she reached her front steps with Sophie panting beside her. They'd run from the edge of the park back home. She felt invigorated as she bent over, sucking fresh air into her lungs. She was happy she had plans for the day, which didn't often happen on a Saturday.

Listening to the girls last night talking about intimate times made Marianne realize that she'd miss out entirely on having kids with no man in her life, something she very much wanted. She'd been cancer-free for two years now, and the doctor had told her not to let life slip away from doing all she wanted to do. He'd said that not to scare her into thinking her life was short-lived. Instead, he said what he had was because he had good reason to believe she'd be cancer-free for the rest of her life if she began to enjoy life rather than worry about it. She knew he was right.

Her thoughts turned to the man whom Marianne was expected to marry … according to her deceased aunt. Maybe she should give him a chance or at least take him up on his request for a dinner date where she'd be out in public and not obligated to have him inside her home. Now that she had girlfriends in her life, maybe she would get their input.

She shook free her sense that something was going to happen that would change her life forever, and she hoped she'd be up to handling whatever it turned out to be. Spending so much time alone, Marianne had expanded her sense of being and was more aware of her surroundings than most. A flash of goosebumps raced across her body, chilling her momentarily.

Remembering Allison's roommate and how she'd acted last night, Marianne wondered what would happen to Susan if she didn't change her behavior. She was a tease, and that never bodes well for anyone. Marianne had seen what could happen to a person like Susan because she was the one who typed up most of the notes on various abuse and missing persons cases that crossed the desks of the two lawyers she worked for.

She sighed and pushed away thoughts of Susan. Today was her day to have fun with her new friends, and she wasn't going to allow anything to disrupt that. So, when the phone rang, she ignored it.

Chapter 7

Allison puffed her way through the narrow streets, crossed beneath the underpass, and made her way around the Haymarket Farmer's Market, where hawkers promoted their fruits and vegetables each Saturday morning. Earlier, before rushing back to the laundromat to hastily fold her laundry, she'd been there to pick up a few items to last the week, hopefully. Now, she was running late to meet the girls.

She zig-zagged around a group of tourists and kept running. Finally, she got onto Washington Street, and when she reached School Street, she ran up it to cut across onto Tremont Street. Allison saw the girls standing and talking to each other on the corner where they'd agreed to meet. She slowed down to catch her breath and sighed with relief at seeing them still waiting for her even though a crowd of people was already moving toward the center of the park where the concert was being held. She could hear a voice over the loudspeaker talking about upcoming events before he'd formally introduce Cyndi Lauper. She picked up her speed. When she finally reached them, she was out of breath and apologized, "Sorry, I'm late."

Both girls smiled at her, happy to see her. "Just glad you could make it. C'mon, let's get going! We don't want to miss Cyndi! " Bella said.

They moved into the park, bypassing the Boston Common Frog Pond, and when they reached the crowd, Allison grabbed onto Bella's shirttail so she wouldn't lose Bella in the hoards of people gathered there. Then, Allison held onto Marianne's hand to ensure she would stay with them. They excitedly pushed their way forward to get closer to the stage. Once they reached as far as they could go, they turned to each other and grinned. When Cyndi came onto the scene, the three of them screamed with delight with all the other women who were there to see the upcoming star in person.

Talking earlier with Bella, Marianne had found out that in 1983, Cyndi's album, "She's So Unusual," was the first debut album by a female artist to achieve four top-five hits on the Billboard Hot 100. Bella also told her that Cyndi Lauper had won the Best New Artist award at the 27th Grammy Awards in 1985.

Looking at the star now, Marianne was surprised to see that Cyndi was so tiny. Her short, pink-dyed hair stood straight up on top of her hair, and she was adorable. The only song that she recognized was "Girls Just Want to Have Fun."

Bella looked beside her to see that Allison was focused on Cyndi Lauper, mouthing the words as the star sang them. Marianne glanced her way and smiled, happy to be there. Satisfied that her companions were content, Bella turned back toward the stage and swayed to the music, humming the tunes in a soft voice.

Allison, hearing Bella's sweet tones, turned to her and mouthed, "Thank you for setting this up, Bella."

♥ ♥ ♥

When the concert ended, they were as sad as the others to have it end. Slowly they made their way to the outer edge of the gathering. As they did so, they saw a skirmish unfolding a few feet away between a white teenager facing off with a black boy. They halted for a second to see what was going on, and then Bella pushed the other girls forward. "Let's get out of here before the cops come."

Marianne and Allison were slow to move.

"Come on, you two. Let's go," Bella urged, leading the way.

Heading to Downtown Crossing, the girls saw that they were not the only ones to think it was a good idea to go to Filene's basement to cash in on their big sale.

Reaching the entrance, Allison said, "Before we get lost in the mob, let's plan to meet here in one hour. Is that okay with you girls?"

"Sounds good," Bella answered.

"It's okay with me, too," Marianne said.

They chuckled as they pushed their way into the milling crowds of people searching for a bargain. Allison stopped at the first section that advertised brand-named sweaters at a ridiculously low price. Bella and Marianne moved beyond her—Bella turned right to look at well-known watches on sale while Marianne headed for the shoe sale.

An hour later, Allison already had a pile of sweaters in her hand when she met up with the girls. "Which color do you like best?" she asked as she held them up against her body, one by one.

"I think it's going to come down to either the green or the mauve one," answered Marianne.

"Or both," suggested Bella. "It depends what matches your other clothes."

"Cool. Now down to the final two," said Allison, clutching them to her after putting the others down onto a pile of items for sale. Then, she whipped off her shirt, wearing nothing but her bra.

"What are you doing?" implored Marianne, shocked.

"Trying on the sweaters, so you can tell me which one I should buy. Why?"

Bella laughed. "Haven't you done this before? That's the fun of coming to Filene's Basement, Marianne. Look around. You'll see everything here, believe me."

Marianne shook her head in amusement. "You two."

After putting her shirt back on, Allison turned to the others. "What did you find? Anything special?"

Bella held out her arm to show off a shiny new watch fashioned after a Rolex.

"Wow, that looks like a real Rolex!" exclaimed Marianne. "Where did you find it. I want one too."

"Follow me, and I'll show you," Bella said.

When they got to the section promoting the watches, Bella stretched her hand into the pile and grabbed the last one like hers. She barely beat out another lady reaching for it. Immediately Bella placed the box into Marianne's waiting hands. Seeing this, the lady demanded, "I wanted that. Are you going to buy it?"

Marianne looked at the box in her hands. Torn between wanting to please the lady and wanting the watch for herself, Marianne wore a determined look. "It's mine. I got it first," she declared, turning away from the disgruntled woman.

Watching her, Bella and Allison laughed. Filene's Basement did that—turned a shy person into a fierce shopper.

After paying for their treasures, they made their way out of Filene's to seek an outdoor cart selling cold soda. Shopping with crowds of other people, although fun, was not always easy and took effort, leaving shoppers parched.

Allison said, sipping her drink while standing around, "Shall we meet next Friday again, like before?"

"Count me in," Marianne immediately answered with enthusiasm. She didn't remember having a more fun time than she'd had the past few days with her two new girlfriends.

"I'm game, too," responded Bella.

"Then, it's a deal," Allison said.

They parted, each going her separate way, not aware of what lay ahead.

Chapter 8

Once Allison got home, she put away her new mauve sweater in the back of her drawer. Even though Susan was smaller than Allison's medium size, she could wear Allison's sweaters because her large breasts needed the room. And Susan was not shy about being the first to wear any new item of Allison's.

Allison went into the tiny kitchen and pulled out a wine glass, filling it from the bottle of Prosecco she'd bought at the grocery store earlier. She plopped down on the cozy couch and stretched her feet out on top of the coffee table, content to relax. Allison sighed with pleasure. She'd had so much fun that day with her new girlfriends.

After taking her first sip, she heard footsteps pounding up the stairs and was surprised when they stopped outside her apartment. Then came banging on the door.

Too lazy to get up, Allison hollered, "Matt, Susan's not home yet. You'll have to come back."

There was a pause before a deep voice said, "This is the police."

Police? What could be the matter? Susan's face flashed before her. Oh Gawd, what did she get herself into now?

"Coming," Allison hollered.

Opening the door, she faced a large older man with a small, younger woman by his side, wearing identical police outfits. Both wore grim expressions.

"What is it? What's wrong?" Allison asked.

"Can we come in?" asked the male cop.

"Of course," Allison replied with a pounding heart.

They followed Allison inside, stepping over the threshold and closing the door behind them. Allison directed them to the couch where she'd been sitting. "What's wrong? Why are you here?"

"Are you Allison ...Sullivan?" he asked after checking his notes for the last name.

She nodded.

"And Susan Richards is your roommate?" he continued.

She nodded, confused. "Why do you want to know?"

He ignored her question. "When is the last time you saw her?"

Sensing something was terribly wrong, Allison felt sick. "Last night."

"Where?" he asked.

A flash of anger passed through Allison. "I'm not going to answer any more of your questions until you tell me why you're here."

The female cop placed her hand on the man's arm, halting him from responding. "We found a purse that, according to the wallet inside, identifies it as belonging to Susan," she said.

"Ohh, is that all? She's always leaving her purse places; you can leave it with me. I'll see that she gets it," Allison said. "I promise."

"It's not that simple," the male cop said.

"Why not?" asked Allison.

The two cops looked at each other, and the female cop nodded to the man. Despite his burly size and roughness, sorrow crossed his brow. "The purse was found in a dumpster, covered in blood. We think the blood belongs to your roommate. We're here to see if you know what could have happened."

Allison took several deep breaths before covering her mouth and running into the bathroom. She made it just in time to throw up in the toilet and not all over the floor. After she finished, she swiped her hand across her mouth and rose. Then she leaned over the sink to wash her hands and rinse out her mouth.

When she rejoined the cops, she mumbled, "Sorry about that."

"We understand you must be upset. Let's go through everything that happened last night, okay?" asked the female cop in a soothing tone.

After they left, Allison struggled to keep from breaking down. Her nerves were shot from answering the same questions over and over. By the time the police had finished with her, Allison felt there was no doubt that things had ended poorly for Susan. Her heart broke at the thought of anything like that happening to Susan. She bent over low at the waist and tried her best to clear her head as she took in a deep breath. She needed to call and warn Bella and Marianne. Allison had given their names to the police, and they'd be contacting them.

♥ ♥ ♥

As Bella headed home, she was pleased with how the day had gone with her friends. She was determined not to allow Benjamin's departure take away her happiness. After all, she had been the one who'd wanted him to leave, Bella reminded herself. She stopped into her favorite little restaurant around the corner from where she lived and picked up a southern meal of fried chicken, biscuits, and greens to take with her—comfort food.

When she arrived home, she placed her take-out dinner in the kitchen and went upstairs to change into one of her lounging outfits. Then, she came back downstairs and peeked into the refrigerator to see if the bottle of wine she'd set to chill in the fridge before she'd met up with the girls was still there. Somewhat surprised that Benjamin hadn't taken it, she smiled and reached for it. Then, she filled a wine glass from the bottle of her favorite Chardonnay and headed outside to sit on her patio. She'd heat her meal after she'd relaxed for a bit.

It amazed Bella to realize that the house felt as empty as it did without Benjamin and the mess he usually left behind. It was hard to believe he had that much effect after living with her for just a few months. But, she had to remind herself that all was okay if this was the worst thing that happened in her life.

She held out her wrist to admire her new watch and chuckled at remembering Marianne's determination to claim the watch for herself that the other woman wanted.

When Bella heard her phone ring, she almost didn't answer it; yet, something told her she needed to get it. So she got up and went into the kitchen, where she grabbed the handset and walked back out onto the patio.

"Hello?" Hearing sniffling, she demanded, "Who is this?"

"Bella? It's me, Allison."

"What's the matter, Allison? What's wrong?"

"You're not going to believe it …."

"It's okay; you can tell me. What's happened?"

"The police just left. They came to tell me that Susan's purse was found in a dumpster, and it was all bloody. So the cops think she's been injured or worse. Ohh, Bella. I'm so scared. I think she might be dead...."

"Susan, your roommate? Dead?" asked Bella trying to get her head around the idea of that beautiful woman no longer alive.

Allison was sobbing, and there was nothing Bella could do except to give her a few moments to collect herself. Then Allison said, "The cops wanted to know all about last night, so I had to give them your name and number; they'll want to talk to you, too."

Great, thought Bella, not liking the idea at all. She hated the police. They always seemed to give anyone black a hard time. She sighed, resigned to the fact she had no choice. "No worries, Allison, I have nothing to hide. They aren't looking at you as being involved, are they?"

"I don't think so. I don't see how they can."

It's a good thing you're white, or it could be a different story, she thought bitterly. "Are you going to be okay? Do you want to come and stay with me?"

"Thanks, but I'm going to stay right here in case Susan calls and needs my help."

"Let me know if you change your mind, okay?"

Allison sniffled some more. "Thanks for your offer, Bella. It means a lot. I've got to go and call Marianne. I need to let her know what's happened."

"Okay, Allison. Call me if you need anything."

"Thanks, Bella."

♥ ♥ ♥

Marianne left the girls and walked to Beacon Hill. As soon as she arrived home, she flew through the door, grabbed Sophie, and held her up in the air, laughing. The dog barked and yipped, excited with Marianne's enthusiasm and many kisses.

Since moving to Boston permanently, this was the first time Marianne had felt happy that she was living there. It was hard for her to believe that she had spent a day with real, live girlfriends. Growing up, Marianne hadn't made actual girlfriends—the kind who would share their intimate moments with her as Bella and Allison had. Instead, the few females her age who'd passed her aunt's strict inspection had been friendly enough but not anyone whom Marianne felt safe enough with that she could share her thoughts.

Marianne picked up the packages she'd dropped by the door and placed them on the hallway table before leading Sophie to the back. Sliding the patio door open, Sophie stepped out while Marianne went into the kitchen and reached for a wine glass, ready to pour herself a glass of Sauvignon Blanc that was awaiting her in the refrigerator. God! She felt so hopeful that things would change in her life now that she had friends. That is what she'd wanted ever since she'd moved to Boston—a place that she'd been told was great for meeting and making friends without needing her aunt's approval.

Spending time with Allison and Bella gave Marianne an odd sense of release that she hadn't been aware of holding. They gave her greater self-confidence to open herself up to new experiences without worrying about being judged or shamed. She chuckled to herself. Knowing that her aunt most certainly would disapprove of Bella as her friend made Marianne cherish Bella even more. Because of her work environment, Marianne was well aware of the discrimination against blacks and its injustice—something her aunt had never considered.

And who couldn't love Allison's free spirit? Marianne had nearly died of embarrassment for Allison when she'd taken off her shirt in the middle of the store to try on sweaters. But then Marianne looked around and saw other women partially dressed, trying on different clothing items. Allison was fun, always laughing, enjoying life.

When the phone rang, Marianne felt strong enough to tell Jeremy not to bother to call her again. She raced to the phone, picked up the headset, and said in a determined tone, "I told you that I'm not interested in going out with you!"

She heard someone blowing their nose. "Who is this?" she demanded.

"Marianne? It's me, Allison."

"Oh, I'm so sorry, Allison. I thought you were someone else." Hearing sniffles, she asked, "What's wrong, Allison? Are you alright?"

Marianne waited patiently while Allison jerkily spilled her story about what was going on. Marianne was stunned. Susan was seriously injured or dead? She knew Susan was trouble, but to end up like that?

Then Allison sputtered, "The cops wanted to know all about last night, so I had to give them your name and number; they'll want to talk to you, too."

"There's not much I can tell them because I'd never met her before last night, but I'll talk to them," she answered with a sinking heart. *I don't like getting involved, but I'll do whatever I have to for Allison's sake.*

"I don't think you should be alone tonight, Allison. Do you want to spend the night here?"

"Bella asked me the same thing, but I'm going to stay put in case Susan calls or tries to reach me here. Thanks, anyhow."

"That's what friends are for. Call me if you need anything, okay?"

"Thanks, Marianne."

Chapter 9

Allison lay awake most of the night with thoughts of Susan spinning in her head. She thought back to what she'd told the police about Susan and what had happened Friday night. When she'd been asked by the cops the reason Susan had upset the man who'd joined them for drinks, Allison had answered that Susan hadn't always realized that her easy dismissal of someone didn't always sit well with them.

The female cop had raised her eyebrow and studied Allison carefully. "Did that happen often?" she asked.

Allison shrugged her shoulders. "Quite often, I guess," Allison responded.

"Did that upset you?" pursued the cop.

"What do you mean?" asked Allison. The cop continued to stare at her. "Listen, Susan was Susan.

Anyone who knew her well wasn't surprised when she acted that way. She did it to everyone and didn't do it intentionally if that's what you mean."

The older cop was looking at a photo of Susan. "She's a real "looker"—a beauty. I imagine she had her choice of men...."

Allison shrugged but remained quiet as she tried to catch the tears falling into her already sopping tissue. She certainly wasn't going to tell the cops just how many men that might include.

"Did her exceptional good looks bother you? Did you two get along alright?" asked the younger cop, eying her.

"I don't know what you're getting at, but Susan and I have been best friends since grade school. We love each other like sisters," Allison sniffled. "Please find her; I beg of you."

As Allison began to sob, the cop was quiet. Then, she turned to the older one. "What do you think? Enough for tonight?"

"We may have to ask you to come down to the station for more questioning. Until we find out what happened to Susan, we need you to remain in Boston. If you think of anything else that might be important, call us immediately, understand?"

Allison, numb with disbelief at what was happening, nodded. "Will you call me as soon as you find Susan?"

"We'll do our best," the older one promised.

When the cops stood to leave, the younger one asked, "Are you going to be okay?"

Allison simply stared at her. "I doubt I'll ever be okay again," Allison answered honestly.

♥ ♥ ♥

Last night, after Bella hung up the phone from talking with Allison, she'd sat down in her seat and contemplated what had happened. Her thoughts went back to a woman at work, also black, who'd warned her that white girls could be a hot mess, and perhaps she'd better think twice about getting mixed up with her new friends. For a few seconds, Bella considered what her co-worker had said. Then, taking in a deep breath, she decided that nothing was going to deter her from developing her friendship with Allison and Marianne. It was as if they were meant to be friends, a feeling she couldn't seem to shake. She'd read somewhere that many times people who lived together in previous lifetimes often came back to be friends or family in another one.

Then Bella honed in on the problem at hand. What could she say to the police about Susan? Yes, she was beautiful if you liked the seductive shape of big boobs, no hips, and long legs. Susan's face was pretty; there was no doubt about it. But if you looked closely, it was easy to see her sense of entitlement outweighed her beauty, and Bella had not been impressed. Yet she didn't know a man alive who would let that stand in the way of his pursuing her.

As Allison said they would, the police had called her last night to meet with her this morning. Instead of meeting at the station, they would come to Bella's house, making it a little less stressful for her. However, when the doorbell rang, Bella's heart pumped with nervousness and fear as she went to greet the police.

Bella forced herself to be calm as she let them in—an older male and a younger female, dressed in identical uniforms. "Please have a seat. Can I get you water?"

Both cops shook their heads. The older one took over and ordered, "Have a seat yourself and tell us what happened last Friday night."

Bella flushed at his brusqueness. Had he forgotten he was a guest in *her* home? Then, pushing her annoyance aside, she began her story. When she finished, the younger cop said, "Tell us about the man who joined you."

"He was someone who had been sitting at the pub. When he heard us laughing, he asked if he could join us at the table."

"What was his name?"

"I have no idea. The man was only interested in Susan, so there wasn't much opportunity for the usual talk around the table."

"That seems odd that you'd have someone join you without introductions," the older cop said.

Bella shrugged her shoulders and said nothing.

"We understand that he was pretty upset when Susan left. Would you agree with that statement?"

"Yes," she answered, not wanting to divulge more.

The cops looked between them, flashing an understanding unknown to Bella. "Thank you. We'll be in touch if we need to talk to you further," the younger cop said as she stood to leave.

Bella walked them to the door and closed it behind them with relief at their leaving. However, a feeling came over her that she hadn't seen the last of them. She pushed that worry away and rushed to gather her things to head out for her shift at the hospital.

♥ ♥ ♥

Marianne awoke with dread. She'd had a miserable night of worry and little sleep. Because of her job, she knew that dealing in any matter with the police wasn't as simple as it could be. Statements could quickly get twisted, and things said could get out of context, leaving the interviewee scrambling to correct the situation. To say that she wasn't looking forward to being interviewed by the police was an understatement. She couldn't wait for it to be over.

What could she say about Susan? Susan's beauty had bowled her over. She had never met anyone as gorgeous as Susan. Yet, something about her attitude, assuming everyone would be excited to be in Susan's presence, had put her off. That assumption of Susan's was disturbing in a way she couldn't put her finger on. At first, Allison looked put out upon seeing Susan, but after that flash of annoyance had passed, Allison's look had changed to one of affection. Having had no siblings, Marianne wondered if friends, who acted more like sisters, always reacted this way.

She hurriedly took a shower and dressed, ready to meet with the police who'd agreed to come to her house instead of having her go to the station. She called the office to use one of her sick days and was grateful not to have everyone know her business. When the doorbell rang, Marianne hurried to let the police inside. She was surprised to see that the younger cop was a woman while the giant older cop was a man. An odd combination.

"Come on in, please," she invited. "May I get you some freshly brewed coffee?"

Both cops nodded, and she led them into the kitchen. After pouring their coffee and handing it to them, Marianne walked to the table in the eating nook. "We can sit over here."

They settled into the chairs, and the younger cop said, "I like how you decorated the kitchen. Very nice."

The older cop cleared his throat, wanting to get to the heart of the matter, and asked, "So, tell us about Friday night. How long have you known the other two women?"

"I met them a while ago. Why?" Marianne answered impatiently.

The younger cop placed her hand on the other cop's arm. "Was Friday night the first time you had met Susan?"

"Yes," Marianne answered.

"I understand from your friends that when she left, the man who had joined your table wasn't happy. Tell me about him."

"There isn't much to say. He was there for Susan, and we didn't get a chance to talk. I don't even know his name."

"How did the man act when Susan left?"

"He was angry," Marianne answered.

"Did Susan say anything when she left?"

"She told Allison not to wait up for her."

"Can you think of anything else that was said or done that might be important to us finding Susan?"

"I'm sorry, I can't," stated Marianne.

The older cop was studying her. "What did you think of Susan?"

His question startled Marianne because she had worried he'd ask her that, and if she were honest, she'd have to say that she wasn't impressed with the person behind her beauty. There was no way she could put that feeling into words that didn't sound as if she were envious. "I didn't spend enough time with her to come up with an opinion," she answered.

The older cop studied her, and to Marianne's annoyance, she felt her face heat.

"Okay then," the younger cop said. "That's it for now. However, we might need to speak with you again. And if anything else comes to mind, please let us know right away!"

Marianne rose from her seat and led the way to the front door. Closing it behind the cops, she took a deep breath. She knew this wasn't the end of it. *All three of us are going to be pulled into this. Just wait and see.*

Chapter 10

Monday mornings were a drag for Allison. It was difficult for her to look forward to the week ahead when like a small child, she eagerly checked off each day until Friday came, and the weekend was on its way. Although she had a degree in Business Finance, Allison had yet to find a job that excited her. That'd caused her to jump from one position to another, hoping to find satisfaction and stability in a position with longevity.

As she was thinking how fortunate she was not to have a job at the moment, the house phone rang, and her heart pounded as she went to answer it. *God! Please, please, please, let it be Susan!*

"Susan? Is that you?" she yelled into the phone.

The silence on the other end was deafening.

"Hello? Hello? Who is this?" demanded Allison, frantic.

"I'm calling for Allison Sullivan. Is she there?" came a professional voice.

"I'm Allison," she answered.

"This is June Slovich calling from the First National Bank to tell you that we have chosen you to be our new loan officer. Congratulations!"

Allison was speechless. How could she tell the bank that she couldn't possibly accept the offer—that she needed to be here at the apartment in case Susan needed her help.

"Allison? Are you there?" asked the same voice as before.

"Yes. Yes, I am. I'm just surprised to hear from you."

"We've scheduled your orientation class for Wednesday at 9 o'clock. You'll be filling out paperwork and reviewing the various forms you'll be using for prospective customers. We're happy to have you aboard."

"But?" Allison questioned, torn between accepting the position, knowing that she needed the money.

"Yes?" asked June.

"Nothing. I'll see you then," Allison said without enthusiasm. "Thank you," she added.

Allison simply shook her head in dismay when she got off the phone. She knew that the Universe had its own sense of humor ... wasn't she experiencing it right now? Just when she didn't want a job, she had landed one. The more she thought about her new position, the more she was grateful to have something to keep her mind away from worrying about Susan. *What the hell had happened to her?* Her eyes flooded with tears. *Who could have harmed her—and why?*

♥ ♥ ♥

Bella was restless. The extent of worrying about Susan and how the other girls were coping was beginning to take a toll on her. She hadn't slept in days, and she had been short with two of her patients when they'd refused to do as she'd asked. That was something she never wanted to have happened. The kids deserved better than that from their doctor.

As if that weren't enough, Mondays weren't easy for Bella because often, she'd return to work after a day or two off to find one of her patients not doing well or, worse, no longer there. And that broke her heart. So not ready to catch up on any news, she avoided the nurses' station and their gossip and tiptoed into the doctors' lounge. When she entered, she came face to face with the television flashing a photo of Susan. Unfortunately, the sound was too low to hear what they were saying, so she raced to turn up the volume, startling the doctor sitting there. As she listened to what was said, she became upset that nothing was new. *Susan was still missing, and no one knew what'd happened?*

She needed to call Allison. They had talked on the phone, but it wasn't the same as being in person. She needed to see for herself that she and Marianne were doing okay. Maybe she'd ask them to join her at her townhouse for a drink and a simple dinner tonight after work. *Yes,* she thought, *that's what I'll do.*

♥ ♥ ♥

Usually, Marianne looked forward to her work week, more out of habit and routine than anything else. But she was worried about Allison, making it difficult to concentrate on her workload.

When she'd talked with Allison the night before, Marianne could hear the desperation in Allison's voice, and she'd felt for her. It was difficult for Marianne to imagine what Allison was going through, especially since she'd never been as close to another person as Allison had been with Susan. But now, all Marianne could think about was that Allison wasn't safe being alone in her apartment. It was a feeling she couldn't shake, and it worried her.

When she picked up the ringing desk phone, Marianne expected it to be one of her bosses who was away on business. They often relied upon her to do extra little errands if need be. Although she hated being the "errand girl," she accepted it as part of her job. When the receptionist announced that Miss Bella was on the phone for her, she answered with anticipation. "What's up, Bella? Any news?"

"Don't I wish! No news, but I thought I'd ask you and Allison to join me at my house for drinks and a simple dinner. Can I count you in?"

"Absolutely. What can I bring?"

"How about a bottle of wine of your choice?"

"Sure. What time?"

"Does 6 o'clock work for you?"

"That's perfect. Give me your address, and I'll see you then."

"Okay, good. I'm calling Allison now. See you later."

Chapter 11

Allison made her way onto the orange line and searched for an empty seat. Spotting one, she moved toward it only to be blocked by a younger girl who scooted in front of her, pleased with herself for having reached it first. Usually, Allison would have made a snide remark, but she remained silent, staring at the girl without seeing her. She was having trouble concentrating on anything since her thoughts had been overtaken with worry about Susan.

Allison became unbalanced as someone bumped into her. Annoyed at being pushed, she turned, ready to snap at the person only to recognize Matt, Susan's recent boyfriend, standing there. He looked as surprised to see her as she was to see him standing there.

Immediately he turned and began to push into the crowd, away from her. But he wasn't quick enough to avoid Allison pulling on his sleeve, causing him to face her. "Wait up, Matt! I want to talk to you!"

People were looking their way, and wary of their stares, he waved her quiet. "What station are you getting off?"

"Roxbury," she answered.

"Okay. I'll get off there too."

Within minutes they heard "Roxbury Station!" called out on the voice system as the car they were riding in jerked to a squealing halt. After coming to a complete stop, Allison and Matt pushed their way out of the train away from the crowd.

"So?" asked Allison. "What do you know about what happened to Susan?"

Matt looked defiant when he spoke. "Listen, I don't know anything about what happened to her."

"Do you have any idea who she was going to meet?"

He shook his head. "Nope."

Shaking her head in frustration, she asked, "What do you think could have happened to her, Matt?"

He grabbed Allison's upper arm, pulling her closer to him. "She was a tease, Allison. Anything could have happened."

"Ow! You're hurting me, Matt!"

He lessened his grip. "Sorry, Allison." He looked troubled. "I loved her."

Seeing the hurt and confusion in his eyes, Allison placed her hand on his shoulder and replied, "I understand."

"Do you?" he demanded, pushing her hand away. "I loved her, dammit, and now she's gone! If only …."

"Blaming yourself doesn't solve anything. I've gone over and over in my head the last time Susan and I were together, and I know I could've been nicer to her. So, don't think you're the only one who wants a different last memory of being with her. It sucks!" she shouted the last two words, causing others to look their way.

Matt remained silent, and Allison turned and made her way forward, leaving him standing on the deck of the train station waiting for the next train. Allison didn't know when she'd felt more tired and discouraged as she made her way to Bella's townhouse.

♥ ♥ ♥

Wanting everything to be perfect for the first time of having her new girlfriends in her home, Bella set out her most beautiful placemats around the cozy table in the small dining area of the expanded kitchen. She was proud of her place and knew how lucky she was to have it. As the other townhouses and buildings in her neighborhood became upgraded, she realized more equity in her house, making her feel more financially secure. Interestingly, that made her more generous in sharing her home with her friends.

When the doorbell rang, Bella raced to get it. Opening the door, Bella smiled at Marianne standing on the top step of her walkway, holding a large bottle of Chardonnay cold to the touch. The clothes Marianne wore indicated that she'd come there directly from work. With circles of non-sleep under her eyes, Marianne looked as tired as Bella felt.

Bella pulled Marianne inside and enveloped her in a massive hug despite some resistance from Marianne in the beginning. Then they fell against each other, pressing close with shared emotions of what they were experiencing.

They heard a noise at the front door as they separated, and Bella hurried to greet Allison. At first glance, Allison appeared to be standing on her own by sheer willpower. Bella's heart went out to her, and she gathered Allison into her arms and comforted her as if she were one of the kids in her care at the hospital. After a few moments, Bella passed Allison onto Marianne, waiting patiently for her turn to hold Allison.

♥ ♥ ♥

Marianne clung onto Allison as if Allison would slip away if she didn't. Earlier, when Bella had called, Marianne's eyes had watered at the thought that she'd see her new friends that evening. She'd never felt more alone by being without them. But, until she had friends, how could she have known how it was to miss them?

Marianne relaxed her grip on Allison, and after placing her arm around Allison's shoulders, she led her into the kitchen where Bella was pouring their wine and getting together a plate of cheese and crackers.

"Let's head out to the patio, shall we?" asked Bella. "Marianne, why don't you and Allison take your glasses of wine with you, and I'll get the cheese plate."

"Sure thing," agreed Marianne. "C'mon, Allison, follow me."

The high-top table had four mesh iron chairs with thick flowered cushions that looked comfortable to sit on. Allison let out a sigh when she sank into her chair, saying, "Oh, Bella, this is so nice!"

"Aren't these cushions the best? Got them on sale at Macy's," she responded.

Then, the girls lifted their glasses in a toast and clanked them against each other. "Here's to finding Susan, and she's okay," said Allison.

Marianne and Bella were quiet, lost in their thoughts of knowing that it would take a miracle for that to come true. Gamely, they clicked their glasses against Allison's and chorused, "Here, here."

Turning to Allison, Bella asked, "What about you, Allison? How are you holding up?"

Tears threatened to spill over. "Not so good, actually. I just can't believe that something bad has happened to Susan. It just doesn't make sense that anyone would want to hurt her."

"The police don't have a clue?" Marianne asked. "They've told you nothing more?"

Frustrated, Allison grimaced and shook her head. "No, nothing."

"Someone had to have seen something. Susan is someone you can't miss," Marianne added.

"Marianne is right. There have to be others who saw her that night." Bella said.

Allison stirred. "Riding here on the train, I saw Matt. He looked so sad."

"Who is this Matt?" Bella asked.

"Someone Susan had begun seeing," Allison answered.

Goosebumps crossed Bella's shoulders as Allison told them about Matt and said he loved Susan.

"I'm sure he has nothing to do with Susan being missing, though," stated Allison emphatically.

"Do the police know about him?" asked Bella, not liking Matt's using the past tense of love.

Allison shrugged. "Matt says he has nothing to do with Susan's disappearance."

Marianne placed her hand on top of Allison's. "Do you hear yourself? It's up to the police to decide if he has anything to do with Susan missing. They need to know about Matt," she urged in a soft voice.

"Marianne is right," Bella said. "I think you need to tell the police about Matt if they don't know already.

Allison looked at her friends and knew they were right.

♥ ♥ ♥

It turned out that Bella was a simple but excellent cook. Each of them gobbled up the chicken casserole as if they hadn't eaten for days. As they sat, sipping freshly brewed coffee, the mood around the table became heavy as Marianne brought up her worries about Allison being alone in the apartment.

"I just don't think it's safe for you to stay there, Allison. You're welcome to stay with me. I have plenty of room and have a guest suite you can use. Your new job doesn't start until next Monday, right? That gives you plenty of time to pack a few things and stay with me for a few days."

"I appreciate your offer, Marianne, but I'm going to stay in my apartment in case Susan contacts me. I need to be there," Allison responded.

Bella caught Marianne's eye and quickly shook her head to let Marianne know to let it be and not pursue the topic further.

"Okay then. The offer stands. If you change your mind, just let me know," urged Marianne.

Uneasiness filled the air, and looking at her watch, Allison scooted her chair back. "Wow, it's getting late. I should be getting home."

They agreed that they would meet again Saturday night—this time at Marianne's house for dinner.

Later, as Bella closed the door behind her new girlfriends, she sighed with frustration and sorrow at the thought of Allison's determination that Susan might still be alive. *What the hell had happened to Susan?*

Why hadn't the police found her yet? Was there any way she could still be alive?

Chapter 12

Allison knew the girls were worried about her, but they didn't realize that she *had* to believe that Susan was alive and would return soon. If not, her entire world would fall apart, and she didn't know how she'd be able to move forward.

Many people thought of Allison as Susan's shadow, but the opposite was true. Susan relied heavily on Allison as her one true friend since her laissez-fair personality and her stunning good looks didn't endear her to many others for any length of time. And because of that, Allison would be like a balloon floating in the air with nothing to ground her without Susan in her life.

As Allison reached her building and trudged up the stairs, her senses became alert as she listened to noises coming from the floor above where her apartment was located. A chill crossed her body as she sensed someone in her apartment. Allison hesitated, torn between wanting to call the police and surprising the intruder herself. Better sense prevailed, and she set her bag down on the top step and bent over to retrieve her phone from her purse. Suddenly, she heard footsteps running toward her and found herself trapped where she was crouched. Immediately, she grabbed for the railing to hang onto to prevent her from being knocked down the stairs. Doing so allowed the intruder enough space to push past her and pound down the stairs, escaping. Glancing at his retreating body as she recovered her balance, Allison saw that he could have been anybody with his blue jeans and a dark hoodie covering his face.

Allison's wrist pained where she'd landed on it when the man forced his way through, and she wiggled it to make sure it wasn't broken. Although it hurt like hell, luckily, it wasn't broken, and she breathed a sigh of relief. Collecting her things from her spilled purse, she climbed up the stairs and headed to her apartment to see what damage the intruder had done. The door stood wide open. Peering inside, Allison didn't see much out of place. Walking around the apartment, all seemed fine until she entered the bathroom. Everything had been pulled out of the medicine cabinet and scattered. It seemed clear that whoever had been here earlier had been looking for drugs.

Allison's cheeks heated at the thought of being unsure whether she'd locked the door when she left to go to Bella's place. Her mind was so filled with worrying about Susan that she couldn't be sure of anything lately. She began to pick up what had been tossed aside and scolded herself. *It's your fault someone got in! You need to be more careful from now on.*

When she heard heavy footsteps mounting the stairs, she quickly ran to the front to make sure she'd bolted both locks on the door. At the sound of shuffling feet outside her door, Allison's heart beat fast. Had the intruder returned? Then came pounding on her door.

"Who is it?" Allison asked nervously.

"It's the police, Allison. May we come in?" came a firm voice.

Her heart quickened as she unlocked her door, letting them enter. It was the same older man and the younger female cop who'd come before.

"Did you find Susan?" asked Allison hopefully, searching their faces. Their expressions told her it was something else—and whatever it was wasn't good news.

"Come sit down, Allison," said the younger cop.

Allison stumbled onto the couch. "You found her, didn't you?" she asked.

"We think that we have," answered the older cop.

"Where? Where is she?"

After a pause, the female cop answered. "A body washed up onto Revere Beach, and we think it might be Susan. We're going to need you to identify the body,

Allison. If you're up for it, we can take you with us now and return you home afterward."

Allison's phone rang, and when she saw it was Bella, she answered it and blurted out what was happening.

"Allison, have you ever identified a dead body before?" Bella asked.

Allison shook her head, and realizing Bella couldn't see her, she spoke. "No, and I'm not looking forward to it."

"Go with the police and wait outside the morgue; I'll join you so you won't be alone. I'm on my way."

As soon as Bella hung up from speaking to Allison, she dialed Marianne to tell her what was going on.

"I'm coming too," announced Marianne. "I'll meet you there."

♥ ♥ ♥

Marianne and Bella arrived at the morgue within minutes of each other. Together, they entered the building in search of Allison and found her outside the coroner's office huddled in her chair, shivering in the cool temperature. The two officers who had come with her stood aside, whispering between themselves, allowing Allison time to be alone with her thoughts. They knew from past times that she needed the space to digest what they'd told her and time to deal with the sorrow she was experiencing.

Upon hearing her friends coming her way, Allison rose and threw herself into the arms of the other women. The three women hugged and cried together until Marianne turned to the cops. "Let's get this over with, so we can get Allison out of here. Ready, Allison?" she asked as she leaned down and pushed Allison's hair away from her damp face.

At her nod, Marianne clutched Allison and Bella's hands, and they gamely followed the cops from the semi-dark hallway into the brightly lit room that reeked of death. Intuitively they turned away from the covered body on the table to steel themselves to what was coming. Viewing a dead person, especially one who had been beaten, was something they knew would be impossible to forget, and they filled with dread.

As many times as Bella had seen a corpse, she found herself having to continuously swallow to prevent herself from heaving. She stood frozen, looking at Susan's body while Marianne stepped back from the horror of seeing Susan's disfigurement and squeezed the hands of the others even tighter. Allison stood gaping at Susan in disbelief, sobs shaking her body. "What the hell happened, Susan? What did you do to cause this?" she moaned.

The female cop approached them. "Allison, is this Susan?"

Horrified, Allison nodded. "Yes. That's her. Does that purple mark on her neck mean someone choked her to death?"

The female cop remained silent as the older cop nodded to the pathologist to cover the body.

"We believe so," she answered.

The girls turned away as one, unable to stop the tears that rolled down their cheeks.

Once outside, the police asked, "Would you three be willing to come to the police station tomorrow to identify the man who joined you at the table the night that Susan had drinks with you?"

"Do you think that he killed Susan?" Marianne asked.

The older policeman held up his hand to ward off any conversation. "Can you make it into the station tomorrow or not?" he pursued.

Numbly, they nodded. "What time?" asked Bella. I can be there in the morning at 10 o'clock. After that, my shift at the hospital begins."

"Ten works for me," Marianne said.

"Me, too," mumbled Allison.

Bella kissed Allison and Marianne goodbye before racing for the train. A taxi pulled up at Marianne's calling, and she and Allison climbed in, heading for the North End and Allison's apartment.

Marianne had insisted that she wasn't going to allow Allison to stay there alone—that Allison was going to stay at Marianne's house for a few days until things settled down. At the moment, Allison didn't care what happened to her, and she was too drained to argue with Marianne. A thought flittered, and Allison realized that she was grateful to have someone else decide for her.

Chapter 13

It was late by the time that Allison had packed some clothes and necessities, and she and Marianne arrived in Beacon Hill by cab. When Sophie greeted them at the front door, Allison was smitten by the adorable dog who danced at their feet. It brought the first smile to her face since she'd learned that Susan was missing.

"Oh, what a beautiful dog!" she exclaimed, making Marianne's eyes light up with pleasure.

"I knew you'd like her. Come on, Sophie, time to go out," Marianne said.

Afterward, Allison followed Marianne up the stairs and was pleasantly surprised at the richness of the house's furnishings. Seeing that the guest suite was as good as any at the Ritz, she let out a rush of feelings that Marianne would be so generous to share this with her. "Everything is so beautiful, Marianne. Are you sure?"

Marianne looked surprised for a moment and then said, "Are you kidding? That is what friends are for. Come on, and I'll show you where you can put your things."

Later, lying in bed, Allison stared at the ceiling and wondered how she had gotten so lucky to have Marianne and Bella in her life. The Universe worked its magic in ways beyond explanations sometimes, and she needed to have faith that the Universe knew what it was doing this time.

Thoughts kept coming to Allison about who would've wanted to kill Susan. What about the man they were supposed to identify—the one who was angry Susan had deserted him? What was his story? And who was the new man she was supposed to meet that night?

Allison strained her mind to ensure that Susan hadn't inadvertently told her his name. Nope, she hadn't.

As hard as she fought the coming darkness of sleep and the nightmares it was sure to bring, Allison's body could no longer function without sleep. Soon, she was sliding into a dream world of her own creation.

♥ ♥ ♥

Bella arrived home emotionally drained after viewing Susan's body at the morgue. During her medical training, she'd been exposed to other victims of assault and had found it so disheartening that becoming an oncologist treating children with cancer seemed a lighter duty.

She wondered about Allison and how well she was holding up because she'd looked so devastated at the morgue. Bella was worried about her. And without a roommate now, she didn't know how Allison would pay rent for the apartment. Yet, despite a history of changing jobs so often, Allison seemed to be carefree about money so, she'd probably be okay, she thought with a bit of resentment.

I always think every white woman has an easier ride in life than anyone black. Who am I to judge Allison or anybody else? You know better than that, Bella Jones! She scolded herself.

Having to go to the police station to identify the man who'd been so angry at being dumped by Susan filled Bella with increasing annoyance. She hated getting caught up in this mess. She didn't like the man—hadn't from the first. One thing good to come out of it would be learning who he was, and was he someone they'd have to worry about in the future? Chills covered Bella at the thought.

Thinking about Marianne and Allison, Bella once again felt glad to have them in her life. She had asked the Universe to open her heart to others outside her job to balance her life in a healthy way. She had no idea that this would mean getting involved in a murder case. She had to have faith that she and the girls would be okay. Bella sighed and turned off the lights downstairs, and headed upstairs to bed. Like Scarlet in the movie "Gone with the Wind," Bella mumbled, "I'll think about that tomorrow. Tomorrow is another day."

♥ ♥ ♥

Marianne climbed into bed, hoping to be able to sleep. Instead, she tossed and turned as memories of the expression of terror on Susan's face became more and more distorted in her nightmares. In a gruesome way, she's become intrigued at how Susan looked lying there on the death table. She'd resembled a large-sized Barbie Doll that had been carelessly thrown down by a disgruntled child tired of playing with it after mutilating its face. Marianne woke up and was afraid to close her eyes again and see the images that had come to her.

She tried to switch her thinking and concentrate on the memory of the man who had joined their table. He was nice looking in a "bad boy" sense, and though edgy, he was not polished enough for her taste. And his apparent anger at Susan leaving him? Wow, that had been obvious. Marianne had noticed a vein in his neck pulsing with it. Was he responsible for Susan's death?

Sophie stirred and perked her ears. She was aware that another person was in the house and was on guard. Marianne listened to Allison crying, and her heart went out to her. She turned to the dog and patted her. "It's okay, Sophie. Lie down and go to sleep. There's nothing we can do."

Marianne forced herself to concentrate on when she'd first met Sophie at the park and all the fun they'd had together since then. Soon, her eyes closed, and thinking of better times, she slept.

Chapter 14

Allison was first to stir. She quietly tiptoed past Marianne's bedroom door and saw Sophie lift her head as she came into view. Allison lifted her finger to her lips and softly whispered, "Shhh." Obediently, Sophie lay her head back down.

Then, Allison continued her way down the stairs into the kitchen to turn on the coffee maker that Marianne had shown her the night before. When the aroma of coffee filled the air, Allison drew pleasure from it. She filled her mug and sat at the kitchen table. For a brief moment, she felt like she was on vacation at a high-end resort with all the beautiful things surrounding her.

But reality soon stepped in, and she shivered at the thought of what lay ahead for them. She didn't like the man who'd joined them at the table that night, full of himself. He had annoyed her from the beginning with his rudeness and lack of courtesy for being a guest at their table. There was no doubt in her mind that she'd be able to pick him out of the men in line with no problem. She wondered about Marianne and Bella's ability to do the same. That night, not wanting to be a part of the shenanigans that'd gone on between Susan and him, the three of them had turned away and tried to ignore them.

Thinking about that night, Allison felt a flash of anger at Susan for being so stupid in how she treated people. *Maybe she had gotten exactly what she deserved.* Aware of her thought, Allison teared up. *So sorry, Susan. I didn't mean that. I'm just so damn mad at the entire world for allowing what happened to you!*

In a flash, Allison went from being angry to sobbing her sorrow. She was a mess—one hot mess!

♥ ♥ ♥

Bella was surprised that she'd slept after everything that'd happened the night before. She'd been exhausted and, if she were honest with herself, depressed as hell by seeing Susan's wreck of a body. It had been a reality check for her. Life was short and wasn't anything to be taken lightly. Giving thought to that idea, how did *she* want to move forward in her life?

She'd been quick to push Benjamin out the door, and yet, she knew she'd made the right decision in regards to him. Did she want a man in her life? If so, as much as she'd opened the door for new girlfriends, she needed to do the same for a man to come into her life. Her new girlfriends inspired her to go beyond her comfort zone and be willing to share herself with them. Why not a man then?

She groaned at the thought that she needed to get moving to get done what she wanted to before she met the others at the police station. God! She was almost sick with the idea of being there. But if the others could do it, she wouldn't let them down. And so, she climbed out of bed to start her day.

♥ ♥ ♥

Marianne stirred awake at the refreshing aroma of coffee reaching her and opened her eyes to the early morning light. A smile played on her lips as she peeked at Sophie and saw her wide-awake staring at her. She was waiting for a signal that it was time to get moving. Marianne laid there for a minute, not moving, thinking that she could take her time getting up since she wasn't going in to work for the rest of the week. But Sophie was not having it. She jumped down from the bed and headed down the stairs, curious to see what was going on.

Pulling in a deep breath, Marianne thought, *"Dear God, give me the strength to do whatever I need to do to get through this mess."*

Downstairs, seeing Allison hunched at her kitchen table, absently patting Sophie, Marianne couldn't miss Allison's grief still fresh with tear-stained cheeks.

"Good morning! It's a beautiful one," Marianne said, trying to lighten the atmosphere as she poured herself a mug of coffee.

Allison turned with a sad smile and nodded. "Yes, it is. Your garden is so beautiful this time of day with all its colorful roses and daylilies."

"Do you want to go outside for our coffee?" asked Marianne.

"Sure," answered Allison, wiping the last of her tears away.

"I'm sorry you're going through all this, Allison."

"Thanks, Marianne. I don't know what I'd do without your support and Bella's."

"You'd do the same for either of us if the circumstances were reversed. We know that. Come on, let's enjoy our time in the garden before we have to leave."

Chapter 15

Allison stood in front of the one-way glass, taking her time to view each man in the line. Right away, she recognized the man who'd sat at their table, but she wanted to take her time to study the others. She was curious to know why each one was there.

Two of the six men were angry to be there—their stance said it all—and it was no surprise that their man was one of them. Another man was scruffy looking, and she'd bet he was homeless, while another one looked like he could have been a policeman thrown into the bunch as the necessary sixth person. The rest were pretty scary looking in their own way.

She felt Bella and Marianne restless at her side, anxious for the time to come to name their man. Until then, they'd been asked to remain silent and not talk to each other.

Soon, the two cops behind them stepped forward. "Ladies?" asked the older one. "Hold up your fingers as to which one it is, please."

Dutifully, they all held one hand open, displaying five fingers. The younger cop and the older one looked at each other and nodded.

"Who is he?" Allison asked.

The younger cop looked to the older one for confirmation before answering, "His name is Carlo Rossi."

"Okay, ladies. You can go now. Thank you for your time," the older one said.

"That's it?" asked Allison.

"For now," he responded.

The women looked at each other in surprise before turning and leaving the room and walking out the double doors into the bright daylight.

♥ ♥ ♥

Relieved to be outside, Bella took in a deep breath and brushed off her clothes. The station odor, which reeked of cigarette smoke and unclean bodies, clung to her, and she wanted no part of it. There was something about the whole experience that left Bella feeling dirty.

Bella watched the other women do the same and noted that Allison shivered in the warm air as if a cold breeze had blown over her. Marianne hovered close to Allison to protect her, and intuitively, Bella understood her actions.

"Thank God that didn't take long at all. Do you have time to join us for a cup of coffee before you go to work, Bella?" asked Marianne.

"I'm afraid not," she replied, looking at her watch. "Call me if anything comes up, though."

Allison stepped forward and hugged Bella. "Thanks for being here, Bella. I know how much you hated doing this."

"I have a feeling that this isn't the end of it," Bella said in a worried tone.

"You might be right," inserted Marianne. "Well, we'll see you Saturday night if not before?"

"For sure. What can I bring, Marianne?"

"Just yourself," she answered, giving Bella a quick peck on the cheek.

As they stood there talking, the man they had just identified came storming out the door, and, seeing them standing there, he came toward them with anger rolling off him.

"So, it's you three bitches who got the cops crawling all over me, is it?" The women stood speechless as he rushed forward. "You better watch your step. No one likes being accused of something they didn't do," Carlo warned.

"We haven't accused you of anything," Marianne said in a low, even-toned voice, unafraid of him.

"That woman was a tease and got what she deserved. She was just another whore like all you women are."

The three stood with flaming faces at Carlo's accusation and watched him stomp away.

"Well, what a pleasant guy he turned out to be!" exclaimed Marianne sarcastically. "And I believe he just threatened us, ladies."

"That he did," mumbled Allison while Bella nodded.

♥ ♥ ♥

Marianne was worried. She knew that neither Allison nor Bella had noticed the photographer snapping pictures from a distance. Had he recorded the confrontation they'd had with Carlo Rossi? Marianne decided not to say anything about it as she grabbed onto her friends and headed down the street with them, away from the police station.

Befriending Allison and Bella had introduced Marianne to a much more casual world than she'd known, and she loved the greater sense of diversity that it brought, enlarging her world. She sensed that all three of them had been thrown together for a reason beyond her knowing.

Intuitively, Marianne knew they'd need to stick together to get past Susan's death and all the judgments that were sure to come their way simply because they'd known Susan … especially for Allison as Susan's roommate. The media always blew things out of proportion, and her work experience confirmed that thought.

She hoped that the media wouldn't label Susan as a slut—something tempting to do with all of her dating experience. That wouldn't even come up if she were a guy, but the standards differed between the sexes ... still prevalent in the 1980s.

Whatever happened, if the three of them stuck together, they would survive, Marianne thought.

"See you two Saturday," Bella said, breaking into her thoughts.

"Be there or be square," responded Marianne. After a pause, she added, laughing, "God, I can't believe I said that."

They chuckled, and Bella patted Marianne's arm. "Not to worry. Call me if you need me."

And with that, they parted ways

Chapter 16

Saturday came with a sprinkling of rain, sending Allison into the doldrums. Noting that, Marianne suggested that they go to the movies, and Allison quickly agreed. They left Sophie snuggling in her dog bed and walked to the nearby theater to watch the film Marianne had suggested—"Dancing With the Wolves" with Kevin Costner.

Marianne explained the plot: "It's a story about a Civil War soldier who develops a relationship with a band of Lakota Indians and befriends a lone wolf he names Two Socks. He is attracted to the simplicity of the Indians' lifestyle and chooses to leave his former life behind to be with them, and they name him Dances With Wolves."

After watching it, the movie inspired Allison to say, "Got to give it to Kevin Costner. He sure is handsome, isn't he?"

Marianne nodded. "He is that. But to give up everything like that? I'm not sure I could do it."

Allison stopped and turned to her friend. "If the right man came along, would you give up what you have to start over again with the man you loved?"

"I don't know. I haven't met one yet who'd make me even consider that," Marianne answered.

"Yeah, me either. But our time will come to find that right man," Allison responded with certainty. "There's a seat on the bus for everyone."

Marianne burst out laughing. "You are so funny, Allison."

"Well, it's true if you believe what my grandmother used to say," insisted Allison.

"Okay, if you say so," she said as she put her arm around Allison. "We'd better hurry so we can get ready for Bella to join us for dinner."

"Sounds good," Allison responded, happy at the thought.

♥ ♥ ♥

Bella was exhausted. It had been a tough day. One of the younger boys had died, and she'd sat with his parents trying to comfort them. Even though his future outcome had been made clear to them, there was no way to prepare for the reality of the death of their child. Parents were supposed to outlive their children, and when that didn't happen, it was a painful aberration from what was expected.

Bella almost called Marianne to tell her she wouldn't be joining them for dinner, but at the last moment, she decided that seeing her new friends was what she needed to get out of the slump she was in. She got off the "T" and headed to Bunker Hill by foot. Walking by the Boston African American National Historic Site, her thoughts turned to what it was like for a black person to live in Boston. Little had occurred to lessen the discrimination against the blacks, and their isolation was apparent by them living mainly in just three sections of Boston: Dorchester, Roxbury, and Mattapan.

Thinking further, Bella was aware that the city was separated in other ways: South Boston ("Southie") was where the Irish had settled, whereby the Italians had settled in the "North End," while many Jews lived in Brookline. Boston was filled with a fascinating history and inequality like many large cities ... not always pleasant.

Bella heard Sophie's barking become louder as she knocked on the front door of Marianne's house. When Marianne opened the door, Sophie leaped forward to greet Bella, who immediately bent to pat her. Smiling, Bella said, "Marianne, Sophie is adorable!"

"C'mon in, Bella. We have a glass of your favorite wine waiting for you," greeted Marianne.

Hearing that, Bella nearly teared up. Being waited upon was exactly what she needed at the moment, and she followed Marianne down the hallway and into the kitchen.

Allison stepped forward to greet her, and one look at Bella's face made her exclaim, "Oh my God, girl! What happened? You look so sad!"

"Rough day at work. We lost a child today," she answered grimly.

"Do you want to talk about it?" Allison asked.

"Please no. I just want to sit and relax and hear what you two have been up to today."

A smile crossed Marianne's face. "We spent the afternoon with a very sexy man."

Surprise crossed Bella's brow. "You did? Who?"

Allison laughed. "Kevin Costner."

Bella stared at the other two. Then she laughed. "So you saw the movie "Dances with Wolves" then? How was it?" Bella felt the tension float away. That was just the type of conversation that she needed—something that didn't make her think … or remember.

Sitting outside on the patio, they greedily ate the vegetable lasagna that Marianne had taken out of the freezer and heated up. It was homemade and tasted delicious. When they finished, and the table had been cleared, the three sipped their wine, and the conversation turned serious.

♥ ♥ ♥

Marianne went to pick up the newspaper that she'd grabbed from Sophie, who'd been chewing on it earlier. When she'd peeked at it, she'd been alarmed to see a photo of the three of them facing off with Carlo Rossi. She hadn't had time then to read what the article said about them and thought now that they shouldn't wait any longer to find out since they were together.

"I have something to show you, ladies," Marianne announced as she spread the paper open on the table. Gasps followed.

"Oh my God!" exclaimed Allison. "Why is there a photo of us in the paper?"

"And with Carlo Rossi! What the hell?" sputtered Bella. Thoughts of her co-worker flashed in her mind as she remembered her warning to Bella that mixing with white people could be trouble. And here it was for all to see!

Marianne silently read the article, sighing as she did.

"What does it say?" chorused Allison and Bella as they leaned into Marianne, disturbing her reading.

"Wait! Hold on and let me finish," demanded Marianne.

A few minutes later, Marianne turned to them, anger on her face. "I don't know who the reporter is, but if I get my hands on him, I'm going to strangle him! He overheard Carlo calling us bitches and whores, and he's put that in the newspaper for everyone to see!"

They stood silent, feeling powerless over what had been written and was out for the public to make what they wanted of it. Once accused of something, it becomes nearly impossible to change someone's mind about what had been said or done.

"The damn media! I'm not surprised that they want to make this more than it was," grumbled Marianne. "I see enough of this in the reports that I type. The three of us need to have the same story for anyone who asks us about Susan's murder, understood?"

"Besides, no comment, you mean," said Allison.

Bella and Marianne nodded.

"We need to separate ourselves as far away as we can from Susan," Bella urged.

"That's easy for you to say, but I was her roommate," protested Allison.

Bella flushed. "I know, but I don't want anyone to think that because Susan was a sex maniac that I am too," she stated bluntly.

"Susan enjoyed sex, it's true. But she was not without discernment. She was more than a whore, Bella," responded Allison with an even tone in her voice.

"Sorry about that, but you know what I mean," defended Bella.

Allison's angry glare at Bella softened, and her shoulders slumped as she took in a deep breath. "Yeah, I feel the same way," Allison relented.

Not liking any upset among them, Marianne sighed in relief at seeing Bella hugging Allison. She overheard Bella whisper, "I know this is hard for you, Allison. Susan was someone you loved, and I'm sorry you are dealing with all this."

Allison lifted her face as her eyes filled. "I'm sorry that because of me, you two got involved."

"Well, I, for one, am not sorry that the three of us have become friends," stated Marianne, "whatever the cost."

Chapter 17

Allison's first day at work was anything but satisfactory. Because of her picture having been displayed in the newspaper, fellow employees were constantly interrupting what she was doing. Although they seemingly came to introduce themselves to her in a friendly manner, it was evident to Allison that they were simply curious to see the person so freely whispered about in the bank. She had shivered and felt sick when she overheard one woman ask another, "Do you think she murdered her roommate?"

Allison needed the job. Her money had run out, and there was no way that she could stay in the apartment she'd shared with Susan without a roommate to help pay for the cost. Allison knew that finding the right person to fill that spot would be nearly impossible.

But, if she worked hard and maybe got a second part-time job, she might be able to stay in the apartment … at least for now.

Luckily, her new position wasn't that difficult, and unexpectantly, she found that she liked it. She'd always been good with numbers. The only reason she hadn't pursued the field of accounting is that she liked being social—around people instead of being stuck at a desk. But with circumstances the way they were, working here in this department would be ideal for her. And she smiled with satisfaction for the first time in many days.

She felt hopeful. She might be able to get her act together, after all, and begin to straighten out her life.

Allison brightened when a phone call came from Marianne just before closing time to remind her to go to her house that night. They'd agreed that Allison wouldn't go back to her apartment to stay for good until the weekend.

♥ ♥ ♥

Bella was aware that everyone was staring at her, and she tried to ignore it. But ever since her picture was in the newspaper, those who recognized her gawked at her curiously … especially when she was riding the "T." She had even overheard someone whisper to another that she was "one of the bitches in the newspaper." And it was no different at the hospital where she worked. Even now, uncomfortable with those standing about looking her way, Bella left the doctor's breakroom in a hurry.

She was keenly aware that she'd hurt Allison's feelings when Bella had announced that she wanted distance from the whole mess. She was angry at becoming part of an ongoing investigation of Allison's roommate and dealing with the police. Bella wanted nothing to do with it. Yet, here she was…

If Bella had acted the way that Susan had with all her flirting and whatever else she did, her grandmother would have smacked her on the side of the head until she'd cleaned up her act. No one in Bella's family stood up against Granny, and she ruled the roost. If you were smart, you learned early on that it was easier not to go against her. Too bad Susan hadn't had someone like her grandmother to straighten her out. But, if what Allison said about Susan was true, she wouldn't have listened to anyone anyhow.

Bella wondered if Carlo Rossi had killed Susan. She felt that he was angry enough when he'd left the table to run after Susan that night. She'd seen enough to know that men with huge egos like that could be dangerous in any conflict and needed to be appeased before things got out of hand. Her time spent in the emergency room had proven that.

When Bella saw the nurse who'd warned her about befriending whites, she immediately held up her hand in defense. "I don't want to hear about it."

The nurse chuckled and said, "My lips are sealed."

♥ ♥ ♥

Marianne didn't remember getting this much attention in all the years she'd worked for the law firm! Most who suddenly appeared at her desk she didn't know well and hadn't spoken to in months except to nod hello, and now here they were chatting with her as if they were friends. "Hey, how's it going, Marianne?" or "How did you get yourself involved with a murder?" or "Who killed Susan? Is it that guy? You can tell me." And so on.

A headache began to form as Marianne tried to concentrate on her work in vain. A certain sadness fell over her as she realized that it'd taken something extreme, like Susan's murder, for her to receive this amount of attention from her co-workers.

Her mind began to wander. Had Carlo Rossi killed Susan? He could have, she thought. In her mind, he was sure angry enough. Truthfully, he'd frightened her as he'd pushed away from the table wearing a furious expression. After Susan was found dead and there was no doubt that she'd been murdered, the police had questioned all three friends, repeatedly asking whether they thought Carlo was angry enough to commit murder. Marianne never answered their question. How could she? After all, it was ridiculous to ask a question of supposition since it would never be allowed in the courtroom.

Her brow furrowed. Since then, she had learned that Carlo had no alibi.

Society's attention span was not much larger than a gnat's, and Marianne knew that the media would focus on another murder or crisis in a week or two. She felt sorry for Allison. She probably would never get over Susan's murder—would just learn to live with it. For the time left that Allison was bunking with her, Marianne wanted to make it as pleasant as possible for her.

On Saturday, she'd help Allison sort through some of Susan's things that the police hadn't removed. Then the few items that weren't clothes, they would pack up and ship back to Susan's parents. At this point, there was no reason for her parents to be here; there was nothing her parents could do. Susan's body hadn't been released yet. Arrangements had been made that Susan would be cremated when the time came, and Allison would see that her parents received the ashes.

Marianne didn't know all that had been said when Allison had spoken with Susan's parents, but Allison had been unhappy when she'd rejoined Marianne in the kitchen. "It was as if I were talking to them about a stranger, not their daughter!"

Chapter 18

Allison had been pleased when her boss had come to her at the end of the week and congratulated her on a job well done. Having landed her position at the bank was working out for her, and she was relieved to have a paycheck.

Allison felt happy for the first time in days as she marched down the street toward Marianne's place. Bella was joining them for dinner, and she was excited for them to be together again. This evening would be fun … tomorrow was another story, though.

Just thinking about sorting through Susan's things made Allison's heart drop. She was well aware that the time she'd spent cocooned in Marianne's house, she'd been living an unreal reality. She needed to act more like the thirty-something woman she was instead of pretending all that had happened was a bad dream. Pushing that thought away, she headed up the stairs to Marianne's house.

She heard Sophie before she reached the top step. The door flung open, and the dog danced around Allison's feet as Marianne stretched to give her a welcome hug. Unexpectantly, tears filled Allison's eyes, and she became overwhelmed with Marianne's kindness.

Stepping inside the elegant townhouse, Allison felt the stark difference between Marianne and herself. Marianne was more contained and professional in appearance and actions and was financially set. Allison was the opposite—carefree and casual—with little in place to protect her future.

Bella had completed her schooling and had become a well-respected oncologist, and like Marianne, also owned her home. Considering them, Allison felt lacking and wondered why either of them wanted her as a friend ... especially now dealing with Susan's death. She wouldn't blame them if they chose to drop her as a friend.

Allison's disparaging thoughts disappeared as Marianne pulled her along, and when they reached the kitchen, she found a glass of wine waiting for her. With gratitude for being there with her friends, Allison pushed aside her worries and joined Marianne and Bella on the patio.

♥ ♥ ♥

It was Bella's afternoon off, and she, too, was glad to be there with her friends. They had suffered as she had by the terrible scrutiny and judgment given by others during this past week. With them, she could finally let her shoulders down and relax. She smiled as Allison joined her and blew her a kiss instead of getting up. The pinot noir wine from California she sipped was delicious, adding to her pleasure.

Like the good hostess she was, Marianne served hors-d'oeuvres. She passed an excellent soft goat's cheese from France, a hot artichoke dip with garlic pita chips, followed by a medley of olives atop hummus. They each filled a small plate with nibbles and relaxed in the pleasant temperature as they watched Sophie run around in the backyard. As they began to unwind, and as much as they had tried to avoid the elephant in the room being Susan's murder, Bella asked, "Any news, Allison?"

Allison shook her head. "Not a word."

"What do you think is going to happen?" Bella asked the others.

Marianne looked worried. "If the police don't find who murdered Susan soon, it could become a cold case. Then, we'll never know."

Allison ventured, "Do you think Carlo Rossi is the killer?"

Both Bella and Marianne looked at Allison, lost in thought. Finally, Bella shrugged her shoulders. "He was angry enough."

"And was arrogant enough," added Marianne.

"Yeah, I think so too," Allison said.

Sophie began to bark in protest, cutting into their conversation. The large tabby cat from next door was sitting on top of the fence that separated the two yards. The cat ignored the dog yipping at her and concentrated on the birds that had landed in the lone tree that spread across Marianne's back yard. Watching them, the girls chuckled with amusement, and suddenly the heavy air of their worry lifted, replaced with merriment.

♥ ♥ ♥

Marianne was relieved to see the others laughing. She didn't want the heavy energy that had permeated their evening to continue. They needed to let things be. What could they do about Susan's situation anyhow?

A short while later, Marianne said, "I hear the buzzer. It's time for dinner. Bring your glasses in with you, and let's go inside to eat."

"Here," said Allison as she handed one of the hors d'oeuvres to Marianne and handed another to Bella. She scooped up the last one, and they headed inside.

Marianne served the simple but delicious chicken rice casserole while Allison tossed the salad, and Bella refreshed their wine glasses. The wine had relaxed them, and they laughed and told stories about some of the people who'd come to them, curious to find out more about their role in Susan's murder.

"I overheard someone say to another person that I was one of the three bitches, if you can imagine that," lamented Bella.

"You mean people are referring to us as "the three bitches? I don't like that at all!" proclaimed Marianne.

"Neither do I!" exclaimed Allison. "Oh, ladies, I'm so sorry to get you involved."

"None of that, Allison. It's not your fault; it's just one of those things that happen in life. If my aunt were here, she'd say, 'It's not the cards laid that make a difference; it's how you play them,'" Marianne said.

Remembering all the times she'd been left out of parties when she'd been younger, Marianne now understood how she had chosen to follow her aunt's words. She had built a shell around herself, not letting anyone close enough to hurt her. After all this time, it was hard to believe that it was only by befriending Allison and Bella that her shell was beginning to crack.

Marianne tuned into what Allison and Bella were discussing. "No, I want to come and help you, too. That way, you can get settled in sooner," said Bella.

"Well, if you're sure, that'd be great," Allison smiled, getting up to hug her.

Bella turned to Marianne. "Thank you for another fabulous dinner and time together. I'll meet up with you two tomorrow after I check in with the hospital."

They said goodnight, and Marianne grabbed Sophie's leash and handed it to Allison while she locked the front door. It was time for Sophie's final walk of the day.

Chapter 19

The sunrise peeking through the window was promising a beautiful day, and despite what lay ahead, Allison was filled with renewed vigor to get herself settled back into her apartment and get on with her life.

Allison heard Marianne creep down the stairs to let Sophie outside and thought that perhaps Marianne had slept as poorly as she had. She was such a good friend, and to have both she and Bella help her sort through Susan's things was a blessing.

As Allison continued to lay there, she went through a checklist in her mind of all she wanted to get done that day. There was no sense in sending Susan's parents any of her clothes. Her mother had already made that clear, saying that Allison could do whatever she wanted with Susan's things. It angered her to think of the conversation she'd had with Susan's parents. Yet, Allison knew they must have loved Susan, their only child, although they could not easily express it. They had never understood Susan's wild, willful behavior, not realizing that it was a reaction to her not receiving the acceptance she needed from her parents.

Allison jumped out of bed and began packing up her things to take back to her apartment. Looking around the room, she knew that she'd miss the elegance of it. Yet staying at Marianne's had given her nesting ideas should she decide to fix up her apartment or move.

She took a quick shower and joined Marianne downstairs.

♥ ♥ ♥

Marianne heard Allison move around upstairs and sighed. She would miss having Allison stay with her. Watching Sophie's ear perk up at the sound of the shower running, she knew her dog would miss Allison, too.

Marianne mounted the stairs and got dressed into jeans and a worn flannel shirt for heavy cleaning. She hurried downstairs and started frying bacon for breakfast. They would need a nutritious breakfast to complete all that Marianne thought they'd end up doing at the apartment. She was in the midst of scrambling eggs when Allison walked into the kitchen, dropping her suitcase in the doorway.

"Wow! That bacon sure smells good. Marianne, you've spoiled me during my stay, and I'm sure going to miss you fussing over me!"

Marianne smiled. "My pleasure, my friend. Come and pour yourself a mug of coffee and sit down. The eggs are going to be ready in a minute."

She watched Allison heading to the coffee brewing and could see her shoulders weren't drooping as they had been days earlier. Yup, Allison was on the mend, and knowing that pleased Marianne.

After eating and cleaning up, Marianne picked up Sophie. "You be a good girl, and I'll be back later, okay?"

The dog whined her protest but obediently went to her bed to cuddle in.

"Ready, Allison? I guess it's best if we walk, right?"

"Yup. You'll never find a place to park. The weekends are when all the sons come to visit their mamas in the North End and double park on the streets."

"Okay, then. Let's go!"

♥ ♥ ♥

When Bella stepped through the door of Allison's apartment, she didn't know what to expect and was pleasantly surprised to see that it was much nicer than she thought it would be. The exposed brick walls gave it a campy, Soho feeling, reminding her of her only trip to New York City. She'd visited a friend bunking with two other women in the South Street Seaport area that also had exposed brick walls and large ceiling beams.

"Woo-hoo! I'm here!" she called out.

"In here, Bella!" Allison called out from a back room to her right.

Peeking inside, Bella laughed when she saw Allison and Marianne with their arms loaded with Susan's clothes. As she recognized the quality of material and high-end styles, some items immediately caught her eye. Remembering that Susan was a model, Bella stepped forward to get a closer look at the same time both women bent over the bed and dropped their armloads on top of it.

Allison and Marianne's faces flushed from exertion, and they laughed as they greeted Bella.

"It looks as if we're going to have our own Filene's Basement here, doesn't it?" asked Marianne.

Bella nodded. "That's sure a lot of stuff."

"Here's how it's going to work," announced Allison. "There are a few items that I've claimed, and then for the rest, we'll go around in a circle, each taking a turn to pick out something we want until we're done."

"Are you sure?" asked Bella, already eying what she'd pick first.

"Absolutely! Susan would want us to have fun doing this, so let's dig in! You first, Bella," Allison said.

Bella moved some clothes aside until she found the chestnut-colored wrap she'd seen when entering the room. She held it out and then wrapped herself in it. She squealed, "I want this! I love it!"

Next, Marianne chose a cashmere duster, too long for either Bella or Allison. Immediately, Allison plowed through the mound of clothes and pulled out a matching cap to the duster, handing it to Marianne. "Here, this goes with it."

Marianne looked stunning in the duster, and the hat finished the look. Allison's heart twisted when she glanced at Marianne covered in Susan's things and was confused for a moment, thinking it was Susan.

"I love this! Are you sure, Allison?" asked Marianne.

"You're the only one tall enough to give it justice. Just enjoy, Marianne. There's lots more to go through," answered Allison.

When Bella pulled out a sweater in a zebra pattern, Allison squealed, "So, Susan did have it, after all! She kept telling me that I must have left it somewhere."

Bella laughed and handed it to Allison before reaching for another sweater that had caught her eye.

Bravely, Marianne took off her blouse to try on some of Susan's dresses, and Bella and Allison teased her about it until they all were laughing.

They acted like young girls, fussing over each piece of clothing they tried on. While one modeled her choice, the other two pulled back or fluffed her hair, trying different styles or pulled at the item to straighten it. When Marianne and Allison touched Bella's hair, Bella laughed at their expressions. "There's nothing quite like Afro hair ... it's always a war to win."

They ended up with four piles of clothes to prove their efforts—one for each of them and one for goodwill. They laughed, joked, and shed a few tears to realize that Susan's life had come to this.

♥ ♥ ♥

Starved, Marianne pulled out her phone and called the pizza place down the street to order food. It was the least she could do after all the emotional ups and downs the day had brought them. Homemade pizza was one of those comfort foods that'd sounded good to them, and they hurried to pull the meal together.

Bella was tossing together a salad, and Allison was opening up a bottle of Prosecco when they heard the front door of the apartment building downstairs bang open. Marianne noticed that Allison shivered at the sound of pounding footsteps coming closer and hesitated to open the door. Marianne lightly pushed her aside, opened the door, handed money to the delivery boy, and took the large pizza from his outstretched hands.

Noting how nervous Allison seemed, she wondered if she was doing the right thing by not demanding that Allison come back to her house to stay. Earlier, the locksmith had come and changed both locks on the door to Allison's apartment. With that thought, Marianne kept quiet.

As they munched on the pizza, they became somber. It was as if Susan's spirit was there, taunting them to find her killer. They all felt it though no one spoke about it. Later, Marianne and Bella took their loaded bags and said goodnight to Allison.

"I'll see you two at the pub Friday night at 5:30 sharp!" called out Bella.

"Until then, I'll check in with you each night, Allison," assured Marianne before following Bella down the stairs.

Allison nearly called them back as she watched them descend. She didn't like being alone in the apartment ... not when Susan's murderer was still out there. But then, realizing it was time for her to move on with her life without fearing it, Allison pulled herself together, closed the door, and locked both new locks

Chapter 20

To Allison, the days sped by when she was at work and dragged when she was home. All she wanted to do when she was in the apartment was sleep. She couldn't get the image of Susan's face revealed at the morgue out of her mind. She was starting to be unable to control her nightmares of different scenarios of how Susan was murdered.

During the week, Allison dropped in at the police station to speak with the two policemen working the case. When she arrived and told the policeman at the front desk what she wanted, she froze in embarrassment as she heard him say into the telephone, "One of the three bitches is here to see you."

Something must have been said to him because he immediately looked ashamed. "Sorry about that," he mumbled to Allison as he hung up the phone. "You can go back," he added, pointing the way.

Allison tossed her head in disgust and opened the short gate to enter and travel down the long hallway. The younger cop was waiting for her at the end, motioning her inside the open office.

"I'm here to see if you have any news about Susan's murderer?"

"I'm sorry I can't tell you anything at this point. We're looking at a couple of people, but we don't have enough evidence as yet to charge anyone."

"I don't want it to become one of those cold cases where no one is charged with her death," lamented Allison.

"I understand completely," assured the younger cop. "We're doing all we can to bring your friend justice. It takes time."

Allison nodded.

"I do have news for you, though. Susan's body was released and transported to the funeral home her parents chose here in the city."

A wave of annoyance flashed through Allison. *The funeral home I had picked, you mean, since Susan's parents couldn't be bothered to choose one.*

"Thank you. I'll let Susan's parents know since they asked me to handle it for them."

A wave of empathy crossed the female cop's expression. "This must be hard for you. I'm sorry."

Nodding, Allison swallowed her sorrow and held out her hand to shake it with the policewoman before leaving. "Thank you," she said in a shaky voice.

Is this nightmare never going to end? Allison questioned as she hurried back to her office.

♥ ♥ ♥

Bella was tired of being pleasant to those who continued to talk about her behind her back. Ironically, by the end of the week, she was beginning to grow used to their gossip and was able to ignore them and not respond to anything said. She had more important things on her mind. Several new children had been admitted into her care, and it was unlikely two of them would make it through the end of the month—always a sad and challenging time for her and the child's loved ones.

She'd checked in with Allison several nights ago, and she recognized signs of depression when she spoke with her. Although she knew that could be part of the healing process after losing someone, she wondered how she could help her.

Marianne had called her the night before to ensure they were all set to meet up at the pub the next day … hoping that Bella was still free to do so.

Listening to Marianne talk, Bella noted that she was becoming more and more unguarded with Marianne, and she liked the feeling that she could trust her. The three of them made an interesting group, and Bella realized how much she enjoyed being a part of it. Being with them was an escape from all that was going on at the hospital, and Bella found herself needing that space more and more lately.

They talked about Allison and the state of her depression.

"No, I think you're right, Bella. To go back to the pub where we first met is a great way to face that night and give us a fresh start," agreed Marianne.

"Yes, let's hope it helps Allison release some of her anxiety and sense of guilt," added Bella. "Thanks for the call, Marianne. See you tomorrow!"

♥ ♥ ♥

Marianne hung up the phone after talking with Bella and sighed with relief. *I hope we're doing the right thing to help Allison out of her depression.*

Her week had been much the same … receiving more attention than usual. But she was learning to go with the flow without letting her shyness or irritation show, and having Allison and Bella as her friends made it easier to ignore what was said about her. She was able to keep up with the demands of her job without letting her mind drift toward the murder. Doing her job well was her main concern at work, and she wanted nothing to interfere with that.

However, Marianne's mind immediately went to Susan's murder during the evenings. All she had to do was close her eyes, and the vision of Susan at the morgue was before her. It was disturbing. So she put on Netflix and sought out different romance or comedy movies to get lost in while Sophie tucked in beside her. The times she had woken up hours after the film had ended, she was relieved to know that for a few hours anyway, she had slept with no bad dreams.

As she twisted in her seat, Marianne was aware that she needed to get out of the habit of sipping more wine than usual and go back to the schedule of one glass of wine with dinner and then take Sophie out for a longer walk than she'd been doing this past week.

She was looking forward to meeting up with the girls at the pub the next day.

Chapter 21

Allison was the first to arrive at the pub. When she stepped inside, her heart lurched at the memory of the last time they were there. Trouble had brewed the minute Susan had joined them. Even so, she missed Susan so much!

The same waitress as the times before headed her way with a surprised expression. "Hi, there! I didn't expect to see you. Are the other ladies joining you?"

Allison nodded.

"Would you like the same table you had before?"

Again, Allison nodded and followed behind the waitress to make her way to the corner table. When she heard heels clicking behind her, Allison turned and was relieved to see Marianne.

"Hi there, Allison," Marianne said as she hugged Allison tight to her.

"Ladies, are we doing Cosmos again?" asked the waitress.

"Why not?" answered Marianne.

As they began to get settled, Bella swooshed to the table and sat down in a flurry. "You're not going to believe it! I heard they arrested Carlo Rossi for Susan's murder!"

Blood drained from Allison's and Marianne's faces. "Are you sure?" demanded Marianne.

Bella nodded grimly.

Allison could barely catch her breath. Although she had believed that he had been angry enough to kill her, something didn't feel right.

The waitress brought their Cosmos and left. The girls toasted each other in a daze—each mulling over her thoughts. They heard a skirmish at the door of the pub. Then, several people rushed to their table with microphones outstretched in their hands. One of the young reporters asked, "You're the three bitches, aren't you?"

One eager reporter from the Boston Globe continually snapped photos as he asked. "Are you relieved that they have arrested Carlo Rossi, and he's in jail?"

Another older woman stepped forward. "Revenge is sweet, isn't it, ladies? It's because of you that he's in jail."

"What do you mean because of us, he's in jail?" demanded Marianne.

Incredulous, the woman responded, "Ever since the article in the newspaper about your confrontation with Carlo, people have stepped forward and have accused him of all kinds of things. If it hadn't been for you three women, he might have gone free!"

Allison, Bella, and Marianne stared at each other in disbelief. The bartender came to their table. "Out! All of you out of here!" he ordered the reporters, herding them toward the door with open arms.

Allison sat, numbed. What have we done?

♥ ♥ ♥

Bella sat frozen. What had just happened? She hadn't liked Carlo Rossi from the beginning, but to be the ones to put him behind bars? She wanted no part of it! Their photo and attached article splashed across the newspaper had set them up as judge and jury for Carlo Rossi? Unbelievable!

Allison shoved against Bella, wanting to escape. "Let me out; I'm going to be sick," announced Allison.

Watching Allison race to the Ladies Room, Bella turned to Marianne. "What the hell just happened?"

Marianne said, "We've got to do something about this. We can't let it remain this way. It isn't right."

"What can we do, other than find that photographer and murder him?"

"Let's wait until Allison returns, and we can talk about it."

When Allison emerged from the Ladies Room, looking ghastly pale, they patiently waited for her to weave her way to join them. As soon as Allison sat down, Bella grasped the hands of the other two and blurted out, "We need to clear our names from having anything to do with this case! I don't want to be involved!" she said in a tight, angry voice.

Allison's eyes watered as she squeezed Bella and Marianne's hands. "I don't either. What are we going to do?"

♥ ♥ ♥

Marianne was deep in thought, reviewing their options. They sat quietly until, ever practical, Marianne said, "I think we need to speak to the policemen handling this case. We need their help to straighten this out."

"Not tonight. Can't we meet in the morning?" asked Allison, too stressed to face the police right then.

Bella and Marianne nodded in agreement.

"Ten o'clock okay with you two?" asked Marianne.

"Sounds good," Bella said while Allison nodded.

"I think we ought to sit here for a while so that we can be sure that the press isn't waiting for us outside," urged Marianne.

The waitress came to the table. "Are you ladies doing okay?"

Numbly they nodded.

"These Cosmos are on the house. Mike, the bartender, sent them over for you. Said he was sorry about the mess before."

Instantaneously they looked in his direction. He was smiling and holding his thumb up in recognition.

"Please thank him for us," Allison said.

After the waitress left, Marianne raised her glass and tapped it against the other two. "Here's to better days."

"Amen," responded Bella and Allison in unison.

Chapter 22

Saturday morning, Allison woke up, astonished that she had slept through the night without nightmares. Looking at the clock, she was startled to see that it was close to 9 o'clock. She hardly ever slept that late. Had she'd taken more than her usual single sleeping pill of late? … she couldn't remember. She needed to be more careful about that.

After showering and dressing, she stood in front of the bathroom mirror. Sweeping her dark hair back in a loose bun made her appear younger and much more carefree than she felt. The jeans and long-sleeved Boston tee-shirt she wore added to her more youthful image.

Although she was glad that the three of them would be talking to the policemen together, what could they really do?

The horse is already out of the barn, she thought—an expression her grandmother often used. She hurried down the stairs and raced into the local coffee shop to order a mocha coffee to carry with her. She grabbed two almond biscotti, completing her breakfast on the fly.

If she hurried along, she could make it to the police station on time to meet the other girls. During this turmoil, Allison knew beyond doubt that the day they had met in the waiting room had been predestined for her benefit. Hopefully, it would be for their benefit as well. Perhaps she'd have an opportunity in the future to pay Marianne and Bella back for their love and support. That's the way it worked most times, she thought.

♥ ♥ ♥

Grudgingly, Bella made her way to the police station. God! How she hated going there! However, she'd do it. She heard her grandmother's words, *"An experience is only as good or bad as you make it."*

"I know; I know," Bella mumbled. She saw Marianne ahead of her walking up to the double doors of the police station. She called out, "Marianne! Wait for me!"

Marianne turned and smiled. "Hi, Bella!"

Bella felt a unique sense of power at seeing how her presence turned Marianne's contained expression into one of joy. Marianne was beautiful when she let her guard down and smiled.

"Is Allison here?" Bella asked.

Marianne shook her head. "Not yet."

"What are you wanting to come out of this visit?" Bella asked, curious.

"I want them to acknowledge that we have nothing to do with Carlo Rossi's arrest. Isn't that what you want, too?"

Bella nodded. "It seems unbelievable that we're involved at all since the three of us had never even met the man before those few minutes he'd sat at our table."

"I'm surprised Carlo recognized us at all since he spent all his time cozying up to Susan," added Marianne.

"Hey, there! Sorry, I'm late," Allison said as she ran up the stairs to join them.

"No worries," replied Bella as she put her arm around Allison's shoulders. "Let's get this over with for once and for all."

♥ ♥ ♥

Marianne took the lead and stepped up to the information desk. "We'd like to speak to the detectives working Susan Richards' case."

"Have a seat, and I'll have someone come to speak with you."

Marianne sat next to Allison on the grubby-aged plastic molded chairs lined up against the beige concrete wall. It was an unhappy place. After ten minutes of sitting quietly, she noticed Allison nervously thumping her foot. Marianne placed her hand on Allison's bobbing knee. "Just relax. It's going to be okay, Allison."

Allison grimaced. "I just don't have a lot of patience." Allison was deep in thought when she became aware of someone standing before her. Allison looked up to see a large, handsome, muscular white man in his early forties, and her heart raced. When their eyes met, a spark of electricity seemed to pass between them.

"Good morning, ladies. How can I help you?" he asked.

"We're here to speak to the detectives working Susan Richard's case," responded Marianne.

"Well, in that case, you're speaking to the right person. I'm Detective James Murphy."

"Where are the other two detectives?" Bella asked. "The ones working the case?"

"Susan Richards' case has been moved to my department."

"I don't understand," Marianne said. "Why?"

"Does that mean you now consider Susan's file to be a Cold Case?" croaked Allison.

"Just organizationally. It's still an active case. Hers is one of many cases we're working on," he responded in a patient tone of voice.

Tears welled in Allison's eyes. "You need to find Susan's killer, Detective Murphy!" she demanded. "No one should be allowed to get away with her murder!"

"We want to find her killer too. We're doing our best," said the detective, eyeing Allison long enough to make her blush.

Marianne drew the detective's attention away from Allison. "We came to speak to you about making sure that our names aren't connected to Carlo Rossi in any way."

His face flushed. "Ah, yes, the 'three bitches.' I understand. We'll do whatever we can, but the horse has already left the barn if you know what I mean," he said in a placating manner.

Allison's attention flashed to him when he used the exact phrase she had thought of that morning. She studied him until Marianne tapped her arm. "Let's go," she said.

Stopping her, Detective Murphy asked, "You were Susan's roommate, right? You're Allison."

Allison nodded.

"We have your telephone number on file. I'll be in touch if we find out anything new, I promise."

"Please see that you do," she demanded before turning away.

The three went out the door and down the stairs feeling that they hadn't accomplished much at all. But like any chance meeting, things were already underway. Allison's face was pink.

Marianne and Bella turned to Allison.

"I think that handsome man is into you, Allison," stated Bella. "I thought he was going to eat you up!"

"Yes, I agree," concurred Marianne. "Who knows? Maybe something good will come out of this, after all."

"Hold on, you two. I'm more interested in finding Susan's killer," Allison protested weakly.

"How are you going to do that?" asked Bella.

"You mean, how are the three of us going to do that, don't you?" asked Allison with a mischievous smile.

Chapter 23

Allison's mind sped. Bella's question needed an answer. Just *how* were they going to find Susan's killer? None of them were detectives or investigators of any kind … Marianne was the one who probably had the most experience through her job of typing reports for her bosses.

"Let's go to the North End," suggested Allison. "We can grab a pizza and beer for lunch and take it back to my apartment. We can brainstorm there to see if we can come up with anything that might help us find Susan's murderer."

Doubting that they could be successful in their hunt but still wanting to spend some time together, both Bella and Marianne agreed to join Allison.

"On one condition, though," warned Bella.

"What?" asked Allison.

"No anchovies on the pizza."

Allison and Marianne looked at each other and laughed. "That's okay with me," answered Allison.

"I don't like them either," Marianne said.

The weather was showing signs of fall. The nights and evenings were cooler, and the leaves were just beginning to turn color. A sudden shiver of foreboding crossed Allison's back, causing her to wrap her arms around herself to protect against it.

♥ ♥ ♥

Bella had to hand it to Allison. She was determined to find Susan's killer. She watched as Allison meticulously jotted down notes about that night they were together with Susan. Bella was impressed.

When they reviewed Allison's notes, Bella asked, "Do we all agree that the first thing we need to do is find out who Susan's date was that night?"

"Yes," Allison and Marianne said in unison.

"A playful smile slid across Bella's face. "Why don't you call Mr. Handsome Detective, Allison? Maybe he'll tell us."

Allison's cheeks warmed. "I don't have his number."

"Well, I do," said Marianne, handing her the card she'd picked up at the station. "Here, give him a call."

With the two of them standing over her, Allison made the call and placed it on speaker. "Hello, Detective Murphy. This is Allison Sullivan. I was wondering if you could answer a few questions for me about Susan's case?"

"Call me Murphy, okay? Everyone else does. What is it you'd like to know?"

"Do you know who Susan was supposed to meet that night?"

Murphy cleared his throat before speaking. "I'm sorry to say that we don't. Everyone we interviewed had no idea either. According to our report, you told the police that Susan said it was someone new; isn't that right?"

"Yes," Allison replied. "Maybe it was someone from the latest shoot she worked. She usually got asked out by someone after one of those."

"Hmm, I didn't realize that," he said.

"Can you tell me where Susan was last seen?"

"You do realize that this is an ongoing investigation, and I shouldn't even be talking to you, don't you?"

"What I realize is that you haven't found Susan's killer yet!" she snapped back. "I was hoping since I knew Susan better than anyone else that we could work together to find out who murdered my best friend since second grade!" Allison said with emotion.

Bella and Marianne looked at each other with dancing eyes and hands over their mouths, trying not to laugh at Allison's outburst. It had been unexpected, and they were delighted to see some of Allison's spunk had returned.

Silence hung in the air. After what seemed like an endless amount of time, Murphy spoke. "I apologize, Allison. I realize that Susan's death must be heartbreaking for you, and without her killer found, it must be an extremely stressful time for you."

Mollified, Allison replied, "Yes, it is. Now, can we or can we not work together to find out who murdered Susan and why?"

"How about this? I'll share with you what I can if you will share with us any information that might be important in solving this case."

"Share with Bella and me and Marianne? That's a deal," replied Allison. "Do you have time to meet with us now?"

"Now? Where are you?"

"In the North End, at my apartment."

Allison heard whispering. "How about we meet with you in an hour?"

Allison turned to Bella and Marianne, who were nodding their heads. "Okay! That works for us."

♥ ♥ ♥

Marianne chuckled to herself when she saw Allison's face grow pink as she hurried to answer the door. Upon seeing that Murphy had brought along his partner, making the gathering more professional, Marianne was glad that they were taking their interest in Susan's murder seriously.

Murphy nodded to Marianne and Bella as he stepped inside. "Ladies, this is my partner, Detective Jackson."

The large handsome black man took them in with hazel eyes that missed nothing, assessing each of them as part of their girlfriend trio. Marianne found that she liked the intelligence behind his eyes and immediately felt she could trust him. Looking at the friendly, boyish face of Murphy and the more closed face of Detective Jackson, she could easily envision their act of "good cop, bad cop."

"Let's go into the living room where there is more room," urged Allison.

Once seated, Murphy said, "Jackson has some questions he'd like to ask you ladies."

As Jackson studied her, Bella's face warmed. She wondered if he was going to ask her the question written across his face—"How did you get mixed up with these two white girls?" However, he left that question unasked and moved on to say, "Let's start from the beginning. Allison, why don't you tell us about that Friday from the time you first woke up?"

Allison closed her eyes, lost in memory. "When I got up, Susan was still in bed asleep. She'd had a date the night before and had come in late. I have no idea what time … I never heard her."

"Was she alone?" Murphy asked.

Allison nodded. "She didn't always bring her dates home. Sometimes, she would go to their place for the night."

"Did you see her before you went to work?" Jackson asked.

Allison blushed. "I wasn't working then. I was waiting to hear if I got the job at the bank."

"What time did Susan get up?"

"About 10 o'clock. We went downstairs and over to the coffee café for breakfast. We usually did that when we could."

"What did you talk about that day?"

"I told her I was going to meet my new girlfriends at the pub where we met, and she told me she had a date that night … with someone new. I never asked her about him, and she didn't offer, which, looking back, was unusual for her. Normally, she'd discuss every detail with me, but not that time."

"Did you spend the rest of the day together?" asked Murphy.

"No, I volunteer at the Suicide Hot Line, and that Friday, I worked the afternoon shift. When I got home to change to meet the girls, Susan was gone. I didn't see her again until that night at the pub."

Jackson looked at Bella and Marianne. "Had either of you met Susan before that night?" Both shook their heads. "And Carlo Rossi? Had you met him before that night?"

"No," they responded in unison.

Static from the radio attached to Murphy's belt drew their attention. They listened to a code indicating an event taking place, and both detectives immediately stood and headed for the door. "We'll have to continue this some other time. We need to go," Murphy said.

Allison closed the door behind them. "Well, what do you think?" she asked her friends, "besides Jackson being hot?"

Chapter 24

Monday morning, as Allison was getting ready for work, her Princess telephone rang, and she nearly missed it. When she'd spoken with the girls the night before, she'd laid the handheld receiver down in the living room, and she raced now to find it among the pillows on the couch.

"Hello?"

"Allison Sullivan?"

"Yes?"

"My name is Justine Wallingford from the law office of Baker & Wright. We need to speak with you about Susan Richards' will. When can you come into the office to meet with us?"

"It will have to be after work. Is five o'clock today okay?"

"That'll be fine. We're located at 101 Washington Street. Just push the buzzer at the front door, and we'll let you in."

"Thank you," Allison said. She hadn't given any thought to Susan's having a will. Many years ago, Susan had mentioned something about having one, but it hadn't crossed Allison's mind until now.

The day dragged for Allison in light of her mounting curiosity about Susan's will and what she had to do with it. When it was time to pack it in for the day, she hustled out of the bank and walked to Washington Street.

Standing in the doorway of the old brick building that housed the law offices, she wondered if anyone else would be there. She took a deep breath and pushed the button to the law office. The buzzer sounded as the door unlocked, and Allison quickly pulled the door open. Stepping onto a thick plush navy carpeted hallway, Allison held back a smile. All the law offices she'd even been in looked the same. Allison made her way to the receptionist's desk, and as soon as she announced herself, she was ushered to the corner office in the back.

The thin, older man sitting there smiled when he saw her. He had a full head of white hair and light blue eyes that were kind. He rose from behind his desk and approached her. "Ah, Miss Sullivan, come in."

Allison searched for his desk nameplate to see who she was speaking with … Andrew Wright, Esq. She smiled and shook his extended hand. Then, he pointed to one of the two padded leather chairs facing his desk. "Have a seat, please."

"Thank you," Allison replied as she settled into the one nearest the window.

"I'm sorry for your loss. I know that you and Susan were close; she often referred to you as her angel sister."

Hearing that, Allison's eyes filled with a renewed sense of loss of her dear friend. "Yes, it's true; we loved each other like sisters," she confirmed.

"Well, I suppose that we best get right to it, then," the lawyer said. He leaned forward in his seat. "I've known Susan ever since she was a little girl. Her mother is my cousin. As you well know, Susan and her parents never got along."

Allison nodded in acknowledgment.

"Not long ago, Susan telephoned me with the news that since she was doing well financially, her parents were demanding that she pay them back the money they had paid for her college education."

"I had no idea! The only thing Susan told me is that she'd had a blowout with her parents, but she'd had settled it."

The lawyer looked kindly at Allison. "She always felt her parents had never really loved her, and after their last argument, her love for them was destroyed. Susan came to me a while ago to update her will and make sure her parents would receive nothing if anything happened to her. So, Allison, my dear, Susan left everything to you—her cash, investments, and insurance policy. She loved you very much."

Allison took the paper he handed to her and felt faint as she looked at the amount of money that Susan had left her. My God! She had no idea Susan had that kind of money and investments. Susan never talked about it.

"But...but...I don't understand! Where did all this money come from?"

"As the only grandchild, Susan received much of it from her grandmother after she passed years ago. Since then, Susan has made some profitable investments. And, as you know, in her line of work as a model, she was pretty successful."

Tears rolled down Allison's face as she sat, nodding her head, taking it all in. A worrisome thought crossed her mind, "Are her parents going to try to get their money from me?"

"They can't legally, but I warn you that they may take it upon themselves to try to get you to give them the money they requested from Susan."

"What should I do?" asked Allison in a panic.

"As executor of Susan's will, I will handle most of the transfer of stock and investments. The cash from her checking account will be coming to you down the road as part of probate, but you'll be able to receive the insurance money right away. Since it is a large amount of money, I recommend a good investment firm, such as the one I use. I'll give you my broker's card for you to call. I know that Susan always liked to pay the rent a few months in advance, so I think that you'll be okay for now. Do you have any questions?"

"I'm overwhelmed. I'm going to have to think about all this. Can I call you or meet with you again, Mr. Wright, to go over things?"

"Of course, you can, my dear. Here's my card," he said.

Allison left his office in shock at how things had turned out because of Susan's love for her. Maybe later she'd feel like celebrating, but for now, her mind remained fixed on how sad Susan must have felt after her parents demanded money. *Poor Susan. I can't imagine what it would be like without my parents' love for me.*

♥ ♥ ♥

Bella began her day in high spirits. The weather was one of those clear sunny days with a cerulean blue cloudless sky and the temperature warm enough with a slight breeze to feel like a soft kiss from the heavens.

As she walked from the T station heading toward the hospital, Bella saw Benjamin ahead of her with his arm around a pretty black girl, and her heart sped up at seeing him. Reconsidering that it was probably best to let them go on without meeting up to them, Bella held back, allowing them to walk further away from her. Suddenly the girl turned around and grabbed Benjamin's arm, pulling him with her as she walked back to a storefront. She was pointing to something in the window of an antique store when Benjamin looked her way. His eyes met Bella's, and he stiffened. He quickly turned away, grabbed his girlfriend around the waist, and led her away down the sidewalk. It was evident that Benjamin didn't want to meet up with her, which hurt. *What the hell? For God's sake, we aren't in high school anymore,* she thought.

Unsettled, she tried to ignore the feeling of being snubbed and get herself in a better frame of mind for what lay ahead. When she got inside the hospital, Bella cheered up, knowing she'd soon be seeing her darling young patients. Bella knew she wasn't supposed to get attached to them, but she couldn't help herself. They were special earth angels—all of them—and she learned so much from them in how they handled themselves with others. They were kind and loving no matter what was going on, putting others first. Right now, she needed to let go of the upset at seeing Benjamin's actions toward her and, like her young patients, remain kind and serene.

When she stepped into the doctor's room, two doctors standing there began to whisper between themselves, and Bella knew they were talking about her. She swallowed her irritation and tried to ignore them as she loaded her purse into her locker. Without speaking to anyone, Bella left the room in search of her patients. Before she reached the children's ward, her name boomed over the loudspeaker, asking her to go to her supervisor's office.

What now? she thought as she turned around and made her way to her supervisor's office.

"Take a seat, Bella," ordered her supervisor.

She quickly sat down and faced her boss, "What's up?" she asked.

"I heard from the President this morning. He received a call from the hospital's Chairman of the Board last night. He read the article in the paper about you being tagged as one of the three *women* (she added air quotes around the word) involved in a murder case and was concerned. He wanted to know if you were the right person to be dealing with the children at this time."

As Bella began to sputter, her supervisor held up her hand. "Don't kill the messenger, Bella. I'm just relaying what was said to me. You are a wonderful doctor, we love you, and the children adore you. I'm just warning that you need to be careful about any more publicity like that. Stay away from getting yourself involved in that murder, and I'm sure this will blow over."

Bella's face turned hot with embarrassment and frustration at being treated like a misbehaving child. She fought to remain silent because Bella knew once she began to protest, she'd say things that she'd regret. She rose. "Thank you for the heads up. You know I won't do anything to jeopardize my work with the children. I love them."

The supervisor stood up and leaned across her desk. "Bella, you're one of the best doctors we have here. Please don't mess it up; I don't want to lose you."

A part of Bella protested against being told what to do. *"I'll do whatever I damn well want to do!"* she muttered to herself.

♥ ♥ ♥

Marianne sat in disbelief. What had just happened?

This morning, when she'd returned from walking Sophie, she heard her house phone ringing, and she'd rushed to get it.

"Good morning!" Marianne sang out.

"Marianne Houghton? Is that you?" asked an elderly southern voice.

"Yes, it is. How may I help y'all?" Marianne asked with a bit of southern twang.

"This is Alma Loveland, your dear aunt's friend, and Jeremy's grandmother," she announced stiffly.

"Oh! Is everything all right?" Marianne asked, alarmed and confused as to why she'd be hearing from her.

"I'm pretty sure your aunt would be turning over in her grave if she knew what was going on."

"What do you mean?"

"I have a subscription to Boston's newspaper "The Globe," and I saw your picture in the newspaper where you were called an unladylike name. And something about a murder? What is going on there?"

"Nothing," Marianne automatically answered defensively. "There's nothing to worry about."

"And who are those other women with you? And a colored woman? Where are your senses, child?"

"Mrs. Loveland, those incredible women are my *friends.* We were there helping the police. That's all there is to it, honest."

"Humph. I told Jeremy that a scandal like that is the last thing our family name needs. I advised him to stay away from you completely. If your aunt were here, I'm sure she'd honor my decision, and I expect you to do the same. Do I make myself clear?" With that, she hung up.

Marianne couldn't stop herself from chuckling. No genteel Southern woman alive would have hung up the phone like that—it would have caused a scandal, particularly in the eyes of her aunt. Yet, she felt a twinge of annoyance at being so easily brushed aside from one of her aunt's dearest friends. It was up to Marianne—and only her—whom she befriended, whether that included Jeremy or not.

Her "senses," as Mrs. Loveland questioned, were in the right place as far as her choice of friends. She knew that beyond doubt because she felt them in her heart. And who could say where their friendship would take them? *"One thing is for sure, wherever it goes, we do not need your blessing, Mrs. Loveland,"* Marianne puffed.

Chapter 25

Two days later, Allison had gotten over most of the shock of Susan leaving her so much wealth. Allison recalled how Susan had given her recurring gifts or paid for a dinner out every once in a while—always done with love, never making her feel uncomfortable being on the receiving end. Allison knew Susan made a good living with her modeling, but she had no idea Susan had the assets she did.

Susan's gift had given Allison a lightness of living brought on by having no financial worries, and she began to contemplate how she should handle the money and investments. After tears of gratitude and joy for this unexpected gift, Allison was ready to share her good news with her friends. She invited them to join her at the Pomodoro Restaurant in the North End.

It was a fancy place with a maître d' to serve and white linen tablecloths and napkins. She wanted to make it a special night for them in memory of Susan.

Yes, for now, she could spend a few hundred dollars for celebrating, but that was all. In time, she would need to move, and maybe that would be when she'd purchase a place of her own instead of renting.

Allison texted Bella and Marianne during a break at work, and both answered YES! to meet at the restaurant at six o'clock.

♥ ♥ ♥

After her embarrassing meeting with her supervisor, Bella had gone home that night, wrapped a shawl around her against the cooling air, and gone out to the patio to review what had been said.

Most people viewed doctors as elite moneymakers and easily ignored the pressure doctors were under when treating their patients. Doctors weren't allowed to make mistakes or cause harm to their patients or have their lives end due to error. Bella prided herself on being the best doctor possible, and it had hurt to have the Chairman of the Board question her worthiness as a doctor to treat the children under her care.

The expression "pride goes before a fall" came to Bella's mind. Maybe what happened was a good reminder for her not to get too arrogant… about anything. Instead of taking offense at what'd been said, she would move on, more aware of her vulnerability.

She was looking forward to meeting up with her girlfriends, curious to discover what they'd be celebrating.

♥ ♥ ♥

Marianne still smarted from Mrs. Loveland's telephone call and laughed at herself when she realized that although she'd moved north to Boston, she continued to be affected by the old southern ways of what was considered proper. The old south would never accept Bella, which hurt Marianne in ways that ran deep, for she knew what it was to be an outsider.

Mrs. Loveland's comment about being involved in a murder brought to Marianne's mind the idea that indeed the three of them were actively trying to find Susan's killer. Maybe she should opt-out of that, not that Marianne cared what Jeremy's grandmother thought about it. Perhaps it wasn't a bright idea to get caught up in that, though.

After work, Marianne had time to go home and let Sophie out and change her clothes. She shivered; the temperature had suddenly dropped, which was typical at this time of year for Boston. Marianne carefully took the cashmere duster that used to be Susan's out of her closet and put it on. She preened in front of the mirror and liked what she saw. As Marianne turned to leave, her eye caught the matching knit hat lying on top of the dresser, and she put it on, covering most of her hair. Then, she left Sophie behind with a treat and headed to the North End to meet the girls.

The tiny restaurant was well-known and always busy. Despite having a reservation, there were times when you needed to wait to be seated. When Marianne turned the corner, she saw Allison and Bella standing outside behind a couple in line ahead of them. Allison saw her coming and pointed her out to Bella. They waved and smiled at her, and she held up her hand to wave back. At the same time, an arm came from behind Marianne and grasped her around the neck. The only thing preventing her from being choked was the hand that she'd raised when waving to Allison and Bella.

Marianne's heartbeat went wild with fear, and she struggled to get out her muffled words as the arm threatened to cut off her air supply. "Get off me!" she yelled as loudly as she could. She twisted to loosen his grip and saw Allison and Bella running to her rescue.

As the man lost his grip around her neck, Marianne turned to face her attacker. The man weaving in front of her reeked of alcohol, and she was sickened by it. "Hey, Susan, it's me! Matt!" he slurred as he tapped his chest in confirmation.

As Allison got closer, her eyes widened in surprise. "Matt? Is that you? You're hurting her. Let go of her right now!" she demanded, rushing close enough to tear him away from Marianne, pushing him back hard, causing him to stumble. She stepped closer to him and yelled, "What's the matter with you? What the hell are you thinking, Matt?"

At her harsh words, Matt began to cry. "I thought it was Susan. I thought she was alive," he whimpered.

A crowd was beginning to gather, and Allison pulled him aside and furiously whispered, "You're drunk! For God's sake, Matt, pull yourself together and get out of here before someone calls the police!"

Matt shuffled away, turning back once to lift his arm in farewell before stumbling his way down the street.

Allison turned back to her girlfriends. Bella was hugging Marianne close, and both appeared stressed and upset.

"Marianne, I'm so sorry. Are you alright?" Allison asked.

Marianne nodded. "It's hard to believe that he thought I was Susan! That's so weird since we don't look anything alike," Marianne said.

Allison said, "It's Susan's duster and hat, and you two are about the same height…." Allison wondered if simply looking like Susan in that outfit would somehow put Marianne in danger. She hoped not.

Bella looked at Allison's sad expression at the mention of Susan. Bella raised her voice, determined to set things right. "All right, ladies, we're here to celebrate. The restaurant is calling for us to be seated, so let's go and have fun!"

Marianne smiled at her friends. "I'm all for that! Besides, I'm curious to know what we are celebrating!"

"It's still hard for me to believe it," said Allison with a lilt in her voice. "Wait until you hear…."

Chapter 26

Allison was busy at work when her desk phone rang. Answering it, she was surprised to hear Murphy's voice. "Hi Allison, I was wondering if you'd have time to meet me for a cup of coffee?"

"Ah, sure. When were you thinking?"

"What about after work today? What time do you get off?"

"Five o'clock."

"How about we meet at that little coffee place near your apartment? You know the one I mean with the coffee cup painted inside the window."

"Is this about Susan's murder?"

"Not exactly," he said.

Allison saw her next customer standing in her office doorway and hurriedly said, "Listen, I've got to go. I'll see you there at 5:30."

Allison's day filled with one customer after another seeking the lower interest rates the bank had just announced. Since inheriting from Susan, she was acutely aware of how best to utilize her newfound knowledge of taking advantage of all the bank offered, and she'd made some changes to her own accounts.

Allison had met with Mr. Wright once and had talked to him on the phone several times. It was a whole new fascinating world to her, and she loved it all! She was so grateful for his patience and help in understanding more about investments and how the stock market worked.

Allison's hopes that Murphy had discovered more about Susan's murder rose as she neared the coffee cafe. She had not spoken to Marianne or Bella about her plans to meet Murphy. Should she have? Too late now, she thought. I'll fill them in afterward.

"Hi, Allison, good timing!" boomed Murphy. He laughed when he realized he'd startled her as he stepped beside her to open the door of the coffee café.

Allison gamely laughed, too, despite jumping in surprise at the suddenness of his being there. Once inside, both stood in line to order. Towering over Allison's 5'3" height, Murphy said, "Why don't you grab a table, Allison? This is on me; just tell me what you want."

She made her way to the available corner table, wondering why he had invited her to meet him. He was dressed casually in jeans, a black tee-shirt under a black leather jacket, and motorcycle boots, making him appear more rugged than the mild expression he wore. She didn't think Murphy's outfit had anything to do with his being undercover for work, but no matter. He looked handsome with his dark curly hair and his eyes bluer than a summer sky.

As Murphy headed her way, she was aware of the other women in the cafe looking him over, and she felt a lightness and sense of satisfaction that he was with her.

"Thanks for meeting me, Allison," Murphy greeted as he joined her at the table.

"Sure. What's going on? Do you have good news for me?"

He looked embarrassed. "Not unless you consider my wanting to spend time with you a bonus."

Allison's face warmed. *So, it was like that, was it?* She smiled. "I guess we'll just have to wait and see, won't we?"

He chuckled, liking her spirit. "So, tell me about you. With a nice Irish name like Sullivan, what makes you tick?"

"Don't you know that curiosity killed the cat?" teased Allison.

"Satisfaction brought him back," responded Murphy, chuckling again while circling the top of his coffee mug with his fingers, eyes not leaving hers.

After two more cups of fresh coffee, they'd shared enough with each other to know they both wanted to see more of each other. Walking back to her apartment building with Murphy beside her, Allison had a sudden sense of loss when she realized Susan wouldn't be around to compete with her for Murphy's attention.

♥ ♥ ♥

Bella thought she must be crazy to agree to meet with Murphy's partner, Jackson. What could he possibly want with her? When she first saw Jackson, he hadn't looked too happy to learn that she was mixed up with Allison and Marianne. Bella sensed that he wanted to protect her somehow and wondered why. Frankly, knowing the law enforcement's history of physical abuse, did she even want to get involved with one in any way. Thinking she might be unfair, she had to remind herself of what she'd seen while working the emergency room as an intern.

Seeing Detective Jackson coming toward her into the pub area of the Ritz Carlton Hotel, Bella involuntarily drew in her breath. He was impressive as he turned heads and made his way through the scattered cocktail tables. He was undoubtedly handsome, and his overpowering physique was threatening just by existing. When his eyes met hers, there was a flicker of interest before it disappeared. Again, Bella wondered why he wanted to meet.

He nodded in greeting and formally asked, "May I join you?"

Bella responded in a teasing manner, "If you insist." Jackson didn't laugh as she had expected him to. "Please do," she added.

A waitress appeared and asked, "What may I get you?"

"Ladies first," Jackson said, waving in Bella's direction.

"A glass of pinot noir, please."

"And you, sir?"

"A virgin Bloody Mary, please."

After she left, Jackson turned to Bella. "I thought it would be best to meet here away from the station. That way, no one will bother us."

"Oh," replied Bella, unclear why that would matter.

Jackson could see Bella's confusion. "Sorry, you have no idea why I wanted to meet with you, do you?"

"Not even a little bit," she responded.

The waitress returned with their drinks. After she left, Jackson asked, "How long have you known Allison Sullivan?"

"Long enough that I consider her to be my friend. Why?"

"We're keeping an eye on her because we think her roommate might have gotten mixed up in something, and I felt I should warn you. We both know how it can look for anyone black to be involved," he stated sullenly.

"What kind of something did Susan get involved in?" she asked, worried about Allison's safety.

"Susan befriended Laurie Naimo, girlfriend of Mafia's Frank Angiulo. Although he and his brother Jerry were arrested in 1983 for racketeering, they're still trying to hold the reins of power in the North End. We know that's changing, and power struggles with the Irish and others taking over what used to belong to the Angiulo brothers are causing killings."

"I don't understand."

"Laurie Naimo admitted to us that Susan thought it would be exciting to date someone in the mafia and wanted her to set it up, but Laurie said she never did. We think Susan arranged a date with someone trying to break into the North End mafia or what is left of it. By knowing Laurie, we think that Susan might have pretended to be more involved with the mafia than she was."

"Is that why Susan was murdered?

"We don't know, but her murder looks like the kind of thing the mafia would do. What better way to demonstrate to the Anguilo brothers that their power no longer counts than killing the 'pigeon.'"

"What does Frank's girlfriend say about this?"

"Both Murphy and I believe that Laurie knows nothing about what happened to Susan."

"Wow, this is mindblowing." Looking him in the eye, she stated tiredly, "I don't believe you asked me here for a drink as a friendly gesture. What do you want from me?"

A flash of shame crossed Jackson's face. "Just keep an eye on Allison. Let me know if anything unusual comes up, okay?"

"Is Allison in danger?"

"We don't think so. But all three of you should be careful now that you have a reputation for putting Carlo Rossi behind bars." With that being said, Jackson laid some bills on the table and turned to her. "Take care, Bella."

Bella sat there dumbfounded by what had taken place. "Damn," she muttered to herself. Jackson was no different than most men she met—they always wanted something from her. Even Benjamin had been biding his time with her until he could reunite with his girlfriend. *What does that say about me?* she thought.

♥ ♥ ♥

As Marianne stepped outside to grab a sandwich at noon, she looked around in confusion at hearing her name being called. Peering around her, she didn't recognize anyone and thought she must have been mistaken. She began to hurry down the street to her favorite deli. Just the thought of a pastrami sandwich on rye made her drool. Her co-worker, an older, married woman, saw her coming and waved to Marianne to hurry. She was one of the few people in the office that Marianne felt comfortable with and was happy to join her.

Once again, she heard her name called, and Marianne slowed to get a sense of where it was coming from. She turned and saw a handsome man reaching toward her, "Marianne, slow down." His face creased with frustration as he urged, "Slow down, will you?"

"What do you want?"

"You don't recognize me?" he asked in disbelief. "Jeremy Loveland III."

Marianne slit her eyes and glared at him, annoyed he'd tracked her down. "What are you doing here? You're not even supposed to be talking to me!"

"Oh, Granny caught up with you, I see," he said apologetically. "Can we go somewhere to talk?"

"Now? I'm afraid not. Besides, we have nothing to talk about as far as I'm concerned."

Jeremy looked nonplused. "According to your aunt and my grandmother, we're supposed to get married."

"Apparently, none of you got my memo ... I'm not interested."

"Can't we at least get together? How about we meet for dinner tonight?"

Marianne's co-worker was heading their way. "Is there a problem, Marianne?"

"I'll be waiting for you at the Ritz Carlton at 7 o'clock. Say you'll be there, please," Jeremy urged.

Flustered, Marianne commanded, "Just leave. I'll see you there tonight, I promise."

"Okay," Jeremy said, turning away from her.

Marianne's co-worker came to her side. "My! That's one good-looking fellow. Is that someone you know?"

"Sort of," she responded. "I'm hungry, aren't you? Let's eat."

♥ ♥ ♥

Marianne was exasperated as she walked into the Ritz Carlton, thinking that, of course, Jeremy would have picked one of the most expensive places to dine. *He's probably counting on me to pay for the meal,* she grumbled.

She stood outside the restaurant doorway, peeked in, and studied Jeremy, who was schmoozing with the waitress standing over his table. Both of them were smiling over something he'd said. For some unknown reason, that irritated her, and she stepped forward to interrupt them.

As soon as Jeremy saw her, he rose, flustered. "Ah, Marianne. Come, sit down," he ordered as he raced around the table to seat her. "I'm so glad that you could make it."

The waitress stood to the side, waiting to take Marianne's order for a cocktail. Before Marianne could respond, Jeremy said, "She'll have a Mint Julep, too."

"Not unless they're both for you," she said to Jeremy. "I prefer a glass of Pinot Noir, please," she told the waitress. "The house wine is fine."

Jeremy's face warmed. After the waitress left, he said, "I'm already screwing this up, aren't I?"

"So far, you're batting a hundred," she responded, holding back a grin.

"Okay, I get it. However, I think if you get to know me, you'll find that I'm not as bad as you think."

"We'll see," she said, enjoying her established power in the relationship.

Chapter 27

Allison was looking forward to seeing Bella and Marianne at their favorite pub that night. She hadn't said anything to them yet about meeting up with Murphy—had simply told them she had news to share.

It was difficult for Allison to envision how much had happened in just a few weeks … from extreme sorrow to a hopeful gladness of living. Every aspect of her life had changed from her home environment to her workplace to her personal life. She was no one's fool, though. She had experienced life long enough to know to enjoy the good moments because they didn't always last.

As she raced away from the bank, heading to the pub, she wasn't watching where she was going and bumped into someone racing past. Her purse was knocked from her, and she watched in dismay as it fell to the ground and its contents spread across the sidewalk. Immediately, she bent down to retrieve them and saw a giant black hand reach down to scruff the items together to hand them to her. When Allison looked up, she saw Jackson, Murphy's partner. "Gosh, Jackson! Thanks so much for helping me. Where's Murphy?" she asked, looking around.

Jackson looked slightly amused. "We're not joined at the hip, you know."

Allison blushed. "Of course not."

"I was just passing by," he said, answering her unspoken question with heated cheeks. He handed her the items he'd collected.

"I'm off to meet the girls," she said, wondering why she felt she had to tell him.

"Okay. Be careful," Jackson warned, causing a shiver to pass across Allison's shoulders.

As she stood, shuffling her things back into her purse, she wondered if Bella was interested in him.

♥ ♥ ♥

Knowing she was meeting up with her girlfriends, Bella left the hospital in a better mood. She realized that a break away from the hospital was much-needed. It'd help to keep her mind off one little girl who wasn't doing well, and Bella was frustrated beyond repair that she couldn't cure the girl's cancer. She needed to remind herself that the closing of life was the beginning of something else ... something extraordinary in Bella's mind. She needed to believe that, or otherwise, she'd go mad thinking that this was all there is?

Bella had thrown the chestnut-colored wrap around herself that used to be Susan's, and upon seeing her reflection in the large mirror hanging in the doctor's room, she'd been pleased with how she looked. It made her feel good as she strutted her way down the street toward the pub.

In the distance, she saw a man who looked like it could be Jackson. She stopped to get a better look, but she couldn't tell. He was too far away for her to go chasing after him, and she wasn't sure meeting up with him would be worth the trouble. She sighed. He sure was handsome, though. Too bad, he was a policeman.

As Bella came closer to the pub, she saw Allison coming her way. An unkempt scary man was approaching her from behind, and Allison wasn't aware of him. Frantically, Bella waved her arms to draw Allison's attention, and as soon as Allison saw her, she raced forward, leaving the man behind.

The man seemed undisturbed by this and kept coming forward. It was then that Bella realized that Jackson had set in motion the fear that something awful might happen to Allison, and Bella could be overreacting. The three girls needed to talk.

♥ ♥ ♥

Marianne couldn't deny it. Meeting up with Jeremy had given her a newfound spring in her step. Not because they had agreed to grow their relationship; that had never happened. But spending time with him had given her a sense of power and the realization that it was her choices that created her life ... not bending to the wishes of others.

Having Allison and Bella in her life now had unleashed her fear to speak her mind without worry or judgment. Something she would be forever grateful for.

Walking into the pub, Marianne was surprised to see Bella and Allison standing by the door, waiting to be seated. Their usual waitress was nowhere to be seen, and Marianne was confused. "Why are you standing here? Where's the waitress?"

Bella looked at her and rolled her eyes. "Why do you think?"

Marianne nudged Allison. "What's going on?

"The new waitress is being a jerk, not wanting to serve Bella," hissed Allison.

"Wait here. I'm going to talk to Mike," ordered Marianne.

As Marianne approached the bar, it was clear that Mike and the waitress were arguing in low voices. When he looked up and saw her, his face reddened. "I'm sorry about this. Please go sit down; your table is ready. I'll have the waitress bring you three Cosmos. On the house."

Mollified, Marianne smiled at the bartender. "Thanks, Mike. Is there any other waitress available—one who has manners?"

Mike bit back a smile at Marianne's directness. He liked a woman with spirit. The waitress blushed under Marianne's glare and, satisfied that she'd made her point, Marianne left, waving Bella and Allison to follow her to their special booth.

Once their drinks were served, along with a large bowl of pub snacks, the women began to relax. Although Bella was used to being mistreated because of her color, Allison and Marianne were still embarrassed by what'd happened.

Allison said, "Bella, I'm sorry for what happened. I guess I knew this kind of thing happens, but until now, I didn't realize how much it hurts."

Marianne nodded her head in agreement.

"Just let it go, alright?" asked Bella, upset. "Now, what's been happening with you two?"

Allison smiled self-consciously. "I met up with Murphy, and it wasn't anything to do with Susan's death …."

"You mean he's interested in dating you?" squealed Marianne.

"Yup. At least that is what he says," grinned Allison.

Bella was quiet for a moment, remembering Jackson saying they were keeping an eye on Allison. Should she mention it? "Just be careful. You know how cops can be …."

"What do you mean?" Allison asked.

"I'm a doctor, remember. Cops have a terrible reputation for violence."

"True, but with a baby face like his, I'd find it hard to believe Murphy would be one of the bad ones," defended Allison.

"Just saying ...." Bella said, holding her hands in defense.

"So, what did you and Murphy do?" asked Marianne.

Allison smiled. "Met for coffee at the small café around the corner from me, the one where you've been."

"Nice," Marianne said.

Allison was self-conscious about sharing with them the intimate things she'd shared with Murphy. So, she changed the subject. "I dropped my purse on my way here, and guess who helped me gather up my stuff, Bella?"

Bella shrugged. "Who?"

"Jackson is who! That giant handsome cop who couldn't keep his eyes off you the day we met him. Has he asked you out yet?"

Bella's face warmed. "It's not what you think ...."

"Ohh, he did! I told you he was interested in you," interrupted Allison. "So, how did it go?"

Bella was in a bind. What should she say? Finally, Bella chose to be forthcoming about her conversation with Jackson. "Allison, what do you know about Susan wanting to date someone in the mafia?"

"What do you mean? Susan wanted to date someone in the mafia? Where did that come from?" Allison asked, confused.

"Jackson told me. Did Murphy say anything to you about it?"

"No, he didn't!" Allison answered in a huff. "What aren't you telling me?" she asked, annoyed that Bella knew more than she did about Susan.

Painstakingly, Bella relayed the conversation she'd had with Jackson. When she finished, Marianne blurted out, "Is that why Murphy met up with Allison—to keep an eye on her?" Marianne's face turned a furious red when she realized how that sounded. "Dammit, that isn't what I meant."

"Alright, you two. Before I say something I'll regret, let's end this conversation right now. If keeping an eye on me is what Murphy was doing, I'm going to kill him with my two bare hands," warned Allison.

"Allison, I don't think that's the case at all," soothed Bella. "He seemed genuinely interested in you."

"You brought up an excellent point, though, Bella. Was Susan involved in the mafia? How can we find out if she was?" asked Marianne.

"Do you know Laurie Naimo, Frank Anguilo's girlfriend?" Bella asked Allison.

"No, I don't," Allison sighed. "Susan was always out socializing and meeting new people, often late at night. For nearly a year before I met you two, I was dating the same guy, and we pretty much hung out at home or the local pub. The local pub is no place anyone like Laurie would be caught dead in, and I can honestly say I wouldn't know her if I fell over her."

"Well, that's that, then," Marianne stated, leaning back in the booth. "Jackson thought that Susan's death was the mafia's doing. Is that right, Bella?"

"That's what he said."

"Well, if we want to know who murdered Susan and it has anything to do with the mafia, I don't think it's possible to find the person responsible, do you?"

Bella and Allison shook their heads. "Probably not," answered Bella, putting her arm around Allison. "Are you okay with this, Allison?"

"I guess I'll have to be. I still want to see what Murphy has to say about this, though," she responded.

The second round of Cosmos was placed before them by the waitress, who said in a small voice, "This round is on me, ladies."

Bella raised her glass, knocking it against Allison's and Marianne's. "Will wonders never cease."

Chapter 28

Thinking that Murphy hadn't been upfront with her about Susan's possible involvement with the Mafia, Allison woke up in a foul mood. When the phone rang, and Allison saw it was her mother calling, she didn't answer it. Although her mother might simply be checking in, she could always sense when things weren't right with her daughter, and Allison didn't have the desire or energy to fill her in. And no longer was Allison willing to have her mother go on another rollercoaster ride of Allison's latest relationship. It wasn't fair to her mother to see her daughter disappointed time and again when things didn't work out. Besides, enough was enough.

A thought of coffee brought Allison out of bed. She wrapped a robe around her and padded her way into the kitchen to brew herself a cup. She poured her coffee and made her way to the small kitchen table overlooking the street below. On a typical Saturday, women with wire pull carts headed to the market for fresh produce and other items. All dressed in black, they looked like penguins waddling down the street. Today was no different.

A sense of contentment overcame Allison as she realized how fortunate she was to afford to live there without a roommate … thanks to Susan. A tear slipped out as she remembered her friend. Then Allison felt a brush of air float past her, and it was as if Susan were right there with her. She smiled and said into the air, "Thank you, Susan."

When she heard knocking on the door, Allison was startled. Edging her way forward, she called out, "Who's there?"

"It's me, Allison. Murphy."

"What do you want?"

"I need to talk to you."

"Well, I don't want to talk to you."

"Allison, please open up."

Flustered, Allison pulled her robe tighter around her and let Murphy inside. "C'mon in," she said as he stood in the doorway, taking her in as if he couldn't get enough of her.

Allison blushed and felt her spirits lift as she liked what she saw standing before her. Nonetheless, she barked, "Why did I have to hear the latest from Bella? You've got some explaining to do."

"I know, I know, and I'm sorry," he apologized, looking miserable.

"You asked me for coffee to keep an eye on me? Why couldn't you have just said so?" she demanded with moisture in her eyes.

Murphy frowned at the remembrance of their time at coffee. "Once we began to talk, that thought went straight out of my mind. I got so caught up with 'us' that I never gave it a thought," he acknowledged truthfully.

Allison's face warmed, but she persisted, "So, what's the deal, Murphy? Why do you think you or anyone else needs to 'keep an eye' on me? What is going on?"

"Can we sit down?" Murphy asked.

Allison pointed to the small kitchen table. "Would you like a cup of coffee?"

Relief showed on his face. "That would be great."

Allison bit back a smile when she saw Murphy overflowing his tiny chair. He looked out of place at the small feminine table with his tall frame and large body—muscular in all the best ways. After placing his coffee in front of him, Allison prompted, "So?"

"The way that Susan was murdered looked a lot like a mafia hit to us, and we wondered what Susan was involved in and if it could be tied back to you. Jackson and I thought we should keep an eye on you, is all."

Allison nodded in thought. "Since I'm not involved in anything to do with the mafia and nothing has happened, what now?"

A grin spread across his face. "Are you free for dinner tonight?"

Allison laughed, her sound musical as it floated in the air. Allison shook her head. "You're something else, do you know that?"

Delighted, Murphy grinned. "I'll pick you up at 6 o'clock."

♥ ♥ ♥

Bella felt an urge to see her father. At times like last night, when the waitress mistreated her, she thought about her father. He always set things to right with his belief that anyone of color should take the high road whenever there was a conflict. He was a firm believer in what Martin Luther King proclaimed. There was no need for violence.

When her father heard her voice, Bella felt the warmth in his greeting, "Hello, my beautiful daughter. How are you, Baby Girl?"

"I'm fine, Dad. I was wondering if I could stop by?"

"Are you okay?"

"Yes, Dad, I just need to talk to you, is all."

"Sure. How about this afternoon around one o'clock? Your moth…step-mother will be out, and the baby will be down for his nap."

Bella knew her father was pleased she was coming. "That sounds good. I'll stop and bring our favorite ice cream, too," she added.

He chuckled. "Please do, and that will be our little secret. Shirley has me on a diet."

When Bella arrived at her father's house on time, he was right there at the door to greet her. A lump formed in her throat upon seeing him. Swallowing her tears, Bella let her father envelop her in his arms. Even though it had been five years since her mother had passed, Bella still expected her mother to be standing by his side and felt her loss each time she wasn't there.

"C'mon in, sweetheart," he said as he took the bag from Bella that she held out to him. He smiled, "I already have our ice cream dishes set out in the kitchen."

She chuckled. "Of course, you do, Dad."

Bella followed him and was glad to see that Shirley still had left most of her mother's decorations in place. Bella wouldn't fault Shirley if she wanted to change them out, but strangely enough, Shirley didn't mind her mother's choices.

Her father handed her a bowl filled with their favorite ice cream—butter pecan—and sat beside her at the kitchen bar. "Boy, I've missed this! There is nothing better! Thank you, Baby Girl."

With her mouth full, Bella answered, "Yrr welcum."

Her father laughed. After taking his last bite of ice cream, he asked, "So, what's going on with you, Baby Girl?"

Bella shoved her empty bowl to the side, beginning to tell him what'd happened the night before, and went on to share her adventures with Allison and Marianne since they'd first met.

Her father remained quiet with softened brown eyes as he listened. When she finished, he asked, "So, what's the problem, Bella? Are you asking me whether you should remain friends with them because they're white? What is it that has you worried?"

Shame washed over her face. "It's not just that. You know how it works out for us, Dad. They have no idea what it's like being black, and for us to have accused a white guy of murder … that's not going to end well."

"Are you talking about the article in the paper?"

"Well, that's part of it," she confided.

"You didn't accuse him of murder. You told me that the police asked you and the other women if that guy was angry enough to commit murder. That's all. Am I right?"

Bella nodded.

"Now about having white friends …. friends are people in your life that make you more than you are. They are the ones you laugh and cry with, the ones you share hopes and dreams with, and they are the ones you will fight to have in your life, no matter what. It has nothing to do with color. Your step-mother is white, and I'm learning that being white isn't necessarily the easy road you might think it is."

Bella's father continued, "Follow your heart, Baby Girl. It will never lead you astray." He stood and kissed the top of her head. "I hear your brother. He's up from his nap, so I've got to go. You are welcome to stay. It'd be nice if you did."

Bella sat in thought. *Am I willing to end my relationship with Allison and Marianne?* Thinking of what they'd shared so far and how they made her life lighter with their caring about her, she knew her answer was … no.

♥ ♥ ♥

Marianne was pumped just thinking about how she was learning to speak her mind without recriminations from those around her, and it felt good. No longer was she bound by the artificial sense of politeness that southern women often displayed. Her new sense of freedom was empowering.

Last night had been an eye-opener for Marianne to experience the lack of courtesy given to Bella because of her color. She had gotten so used to seeing Bella as another woman without thinking of her skin color that having that happen to Bella made Marianne angry just thinking about it.

The doorbell rang, causing Sophie to bark and race to the front door. By the time Marianne caught up to her, the dog was dancing at her feet in excitement. When Marianne opened the door, a delivery man was standing there holding a large florist box in his hands.

"This is for the lady of the house," he said smiling, handing the box to her.

"Thank you," Marianne said, surprised, and turned to go into the house.

Marianne placed the big box on the kitchen counter and untied the red satin ribbon. Peeking inside, she saw beautiful red roses, and their tantalizing odor began to fill the room. Her heart raced with anticipation. Marianne looked for the card announcing the sender and message. She looked down and saw Sophie chewing on it. She bent to grab it before it was utterly destroyed.

The card read, *"I hope you'll give me another chance. Jeremy."*

Marianne felt her defenses momentarily fall as she read and reread Jeremy's message. Her eyes filled not so much to do with his message but with the idea of having received a dozen beautiful red roses at all … the first time of ever having them bestowed to her. It was hard for her to acknowledge that it'd taken so many years before that'd happened … and by Jeremy of all people!

Marianne reached for a large crystal vase and began to trim the bottom of the stems and arrange each rose into the water with the packet of preserver added to it. She bent and sniffed each bud and filled with a sense of pleasure at their beauty. *Should I give Jeremy another chance? Why? Is it going to make any difference?*

When Jeremy called later as she knew he would, he said, "I hope you received my roses…"

"They are beautiful, Jeremy. Thank you," replied Marianne.

"I hope you'll give me another chance." Receiving no response, he added, "Do you like seafood?"

"I do," Marianne said.

"Wonderful. I know a great little lobster shack that is still open. Are you up for a simple lobster bake tonight?"

Marianne loved lobster, and the thought of it alone urged her to ask, "What time were you thinking?"

"How does five-thirty sound?"

"Can we make it six o'clock? I have to feed Sophie and get her settled first."

"Sounds good. I'll pick you up. Remember, it's casual dress."

"Do you know where I live?"

"My granny sent me your address a while ago."

"And it's taken you this long to find me?" she asked illogically, amazed at what had popped out of her mouth.

Jeremy laughed. "Be ready at six. See you then."

Marianne hung up the phone, confused. Why had she agreed to go out with Jeremy if she wasn't interested in him? Sure, he was handsome, but he was interested in her for her money. So, why then? Did she feel obligated to go because he'd sent her flowers? Shaking her head in dismay at herself, she mumbled, *"I'll go for the lobster if nothing else."*

Chapter 29

Allison couldn't believe it had been two weeks since she last saw her girlfriends. It seemed that something always got into the way of their gathering. Extra work at the bank for year-end accounting and future predictions kept Allison busy in her job. During that time, Bella was going through a rough time by losing three children to cancer, and Marianne was dating Jeremy!

Allison had been out with Murphy several times, making her increasingly aware that a policeman's life was not his own. Being a cop was demanding and not always pleasant. Allison had decided not to get attached to Murphy, although they had so much fun when they were together. He was like a little boy who hadn't grown up, evident by his laughing easily at the simplest things in life.

Leaving the bank, Allison slung her bag over her heavy coat and marched down the street with her head tucked into the scarf wrapped around her neck. The wind whipped around the tall buildings and encircled each person brave enough to walk the streets. As much as Chicago was called the "Windy City," Allison thought Boston deserved the title more. She shivered and continued on her way.

"Hey, bitch!"

Allison walked on, ignoring the caller.

She heard footsteps hurrying her way. "I'm talking to you, bitch!"

Allison turned in alarm, facing her teenage attacker. "Who are you calling a bitch?"

"Ain't you one of the three bitches?"

"What is it you want?" she demanded, angry at him for using the nickname earned from her skirmish with Carlo Rossi.

"You have everyone believing that Carlo killed your friend, but he didn't do it. And I know who did."

"What are you saying? You know who murdered Susan?"

Knowing he had her attention, he said with a sly grin, "It'll cost you, though."

Without hesitating, Allison asked, "How much?"

"Well, now, that depends. How much are you willing to pay?"

By now, Allison realized that she was dealing with someone inexperienced—someone who might be scamming her. "If you know who murdered Susan, I want to see some proof."

"Well, I…."

"Just what I thought. You're lying, aren't you?"

"You'll just have to take my word for it, is all. And if you don't, you'll never know who murdered your friend, will you?" he smirked.

Allison stared long and hard at the youth. He had her trapped. If she didn't follow through, she'd always wonder if he knew who Susan's killer was. "What kind of money are you talking about?"

"Five Gs … in hundred-dollar bills."

Allison gulped. "I don't have that kind of money lying around. I'll need to go to the bank, and they're closed now."

"How about we meet tomorrow, then?"

"I guess that might work. I'll have to get to the bank before it closes at noon." At his expression, she added. "Tomorrow is Saturday—short hours."

Looking hopeful, he said in a rush, "Come alone. I'll be able to spot if anyone else is with you, so don't try anything. Then you'll never find out who killed your friend, understand? Meet me at noon at Boston Commons … near the corner of Tremont. There's a bench there underneath a large tree."

Allison nodded. "I know the one you're talking about."

"And don't forget to bring the money!" he ordered before turning and running away.

Allison watched him leave, taking in everything about him so she'd be able to recognize him the next day should he decide to wear different clothing. The entire conversation had taken a mere few minutes leaving Allison feeling drained as if their meeting had been hours long. She needed to talk to the girls to see if what she was planning made sense.

♥ ♥ ♥

Bella had had a few crappy weeks filled with the sadness of saying goodbye to three little ones who didn't survive their treatments. She had heard from her father several times, checking up on her to ensure she was doing okay. Bella was glad he was there for her. She smiled at the thought of him acting more like a mother than he had ever done before.

Jackson had called her a few times, and believing he wasn't interested in her personally, she responded only once to tell him that she had no news to report. Meanwhile, Allison had called to say that Murphy had told her that Jackson wanted to ask Bella out on a date. At the thought, Bella shook her head. *That was never going to happen,* she told herself.

Marianne had called her one night to see if she would meet Jeremy and her for a nightcap at the Ritz Carlton hotel. Although she'd been tempted, Bella had received a call from the hospital to return … one of the children wanted to see her. Bella sighed. Thank

God she had a few days off! She was looking forward to relaxing, shopping, and meeting up with her girlfriends.

Turning the corner, she bumped into Benjamin, her former boyfriend. He was as startled to see her as she was. "Benjamin!"

"Bella! Sorry about that. I wasn't watching where I was going," he muttered. "You look good, Bella," he added, scanning her up and down as he had when they'd first met.

"No worries," she said as the same young black girl she'd seen with him before came rushing to his side. "Who's this?" she asked, looking at Bella.

Benjamin had the decency to blush when he realized that it must be evident to Bella that he'd moved on from his former girlfriend—the one he had recently moved in with after leaving Bella. This girl was much younger and not as pretty as his former girlfriend. Benjamin made the introductions and immediately said to the young girl, "C'mon, or we'll be late to meet your friends."

Oh, Benjamin, what are you doing? Bella asked herself, not that she really cared.

♥ ♥ ♥

Marianne couldn't believe she was dating Jeremy if you called the three dinner dates that. She was curious to learn more about him since her aunt had been so insistent that he'd make her an excellent life partner … love never being mentioned. She was surprised at his somewhat mocking sense of humor about his upbringing. Marianne was beginning to think he might be seeing some of the falseness of the southern ways now that he was living in Boston.

Not to be taken in, Marianne began searching the internet and social media to learn more about Jeremy Loveland III, if possible. His Facebook account looked like it was more for show than anything else, with just a few photos of him and his female cousin who also lived in Massachusetts. He was listed as single and working for one of the larger investment houses in town. That alone surprised Marianne. Usually, investors make good money. Was she wrong about him? Could it be that he was genuinely interested in her, and it was not about her money? She sighed. *Come on, you know the answer to that,* she scolded herself.

It seemed strange that so much time had gone by without gathering with her girlfriends, and Marianne was hungry to see them again. All day she smiled in anticipation to meet up with them at their favorite pub. Grabbing her coat at the end of the workday, she wrapped herself in it and trudged her way through the cold wind headed to the pub.

♥ ♥ ♥

As soon as Marianne stepped into the pub, Mike saw her and smiled. "Are the others joining you? Do you want me to start making the Cosmos?"

Marianne laughed, her beauty shining as she responded, "Yes and yes."

"Okay. I'll have the table cleared and ready for you."

Marianne was glad to remove her beautiful but heavy camel hair coat. It was a chilly night, and the fire's warmth from the far side of the room was welcomed. A few minutes later, Bella plopped down beside Marianne with a sigh. "Boy, I'm sure glad to see you. Where's Allison?" she asked, dumping her coat into an empty chair at the table nearest them.

"Oh, here she comes now!" Marianne said, smiling at the shivering bundle of black coat and red scarf.

Once Allison was standing in front of them, Bella and Marianne said in unison, "What's wrong?"

"You're not going to believe what just happened!" Allison said in a rush.

"Here, give me your coat and sit down," Bella ordered. "Here comes the Cosmos."

Allison's eyes shone with worry. "I need your advice," she said as she knocked her glass against the other two. "I don't know if I'm doing the right thing or not."

"Slow down and tell us what's going on," encouraged Marianne.

After filling her friends in with what'd happened, Bella was the first to speak. "What does Murphy have to say about it? You told him, right?"

Allison shook her head. "No, and I'm not going to, either. You know how cops can be spotted a mile away, and the guy said everything was off if I got anyone else involved."

"Well, we're certainly not going to let you do this alone, without us," proclaimed Marianne.

"You heard what Allison said about involving anyone else. He might recognize us … especially since he already did Allison. I'm not so sure we should be there," Bella said.

"I agree," Allison said.

"Listen to me, you two. Allison, you can't do this alone. You need our help, right, Bella?"

"Well, I think you shouldn't go alone," agreed Bella, remaining silent about thinking it should be Murphy with her.

"What are you going to do? Wear disguises so he won't recognize you?" asked Allison in a teasing manner.

"Exactly!" Marianne proclaimed with a mischievous grin. "I already have a wig I can use. What about you, Bella?"

"I can pretend to be a nun," Bella answered. "I have the costume already." At the surprised looks from Allison and Marianne, she laughed. "Don't ask."

Allison's eyes filled as she examined her friends' faces. "You would do this for me?"

Marianne and Bella nodded. "Of course, we would. You'd do the same for either of us," Marianne said.

"And the money? You don't think I'm foolish to be giving him the money?" Allison asked.

"If you don't do this, just like the guy said, you'd wonder for the rest of your life whether he was telling the truth or not. And, thanks to Susan, you can afford to do it," Bella said, patting Allison's arm.

The three put their heads together, planning what to do if the blackmailer was a danger to Allison. Then, they clicked their glasses again—this time with a common purpose.

Chapter 30

Allison waited impatiently while the bank teller signed off on her request for the large sum of money she wanted to withdraw. She was conscious of the people behind her watching intently as the bank teller took her time to count off the hundred-dollar bills. When the bank teller finished, Allison grabbed the envelope, stuffed it into her oversized bag, and left. She had an hour to kill before meeting up with her blackmailer.

Allison had woken up early and hadn't considered the consequences when she poured herself a second cup of coffee. Too much coffee and she'd have to make a run to the bathroom. And being nervous didn't help the situation, either.

She arrived early at Boston Commons and furtively looked around, seeing if she recognized Bella and Marianne. She didn't see them anywhere, and her stomach roiled. Maybe this wasn't such a good idea, after all. She checked her watch … fifteen minutes to go.

Although it was cool outside, Allison felt overheated. She unwrapped the scarf around her neck and let it fall loose down her front. Feeling better, she again scoured the area in search of her girlfriends. Allison saw a nun talking to children wearing rollerskates down the pathway. The nun was rotund, making Allison question whether it was Bella.

Checking her watch, Allison saw she had five minutes before the deadline. She slowly walked toward the area the blackmailer had mentioned, looking for the bench where she was to meet her man. Although the bench was in the open, it was far enough away from the pathway to give it privacy.

She searched once again for her friends. Allison spotted an older gray-haired woman with a cane resting beside her sitting on the bench catty corner to where she was headed. A smile crossed her face as she recognized Marianne, who ignored her. The nun Allison had spotted before was coming closer, still talking to the children as they skated circles around her. She knew it had to be Bella … children adored her.

Allison made her way to the bench and sat down, clutching her bag tight against her chest. She waited and waited what seemed hours, but, in actuality, was only a few minutes. Then, the blackmailer seemed to come out of nowhere from behind and plopped himself onto the bench, his hand extended for his money.

Allison turned toward him, "You said you know who murdered Susan … who is it?"

"No way. I want to see the money first!"

"Well, *I* want to hear what you know about Susan's death," she countered. "Then, we'll see about the money."

The man inched his way toward and placed his arm around her shoulders as if they were lovers. Whispering low, "If you don't want me to hurt you, give me the money now."

"You don't know who killed Susan, do you?" Allison said, knowing it was true.

He smirked. "What difference does it make who killed her? She's dead! If you don't want to be dead, too, give me the money!"

Allison tried to squirm away from him, but he grabbed her around the throat and began to squeeze. She raised her elbow and knocked him on the jaw, making him lose his grip on her. She yelled, "Thief! Thief!"—the magic words for Bella and Marianne to rush him.

Startled when he heard Allison shouting and saw Marianne approaching, the blackmailer leaped up from the bench. As he ran onto the pathway to escape— Allison close behind him—the four children raced forward on roller skates and began circling him. Bella waddled toward them in her oversized costume and ordered, "That's right, children, make him the monkey in the middle."

As he struggled to get away, Allison threw her scarf at his feet, tripping him just before the cane Marianne was wielding made contact with his head. He didn't stand a chance. Two policemen rushed forward to see what the skirmish was all about. As soon as they made sense of what was happening, they helped the man up and handcuffed him.

"You, bitch!" the young man hollered at Allison.

"I believe you mean the three bitches," Marianne stated proudly, wrapping her arms around Bella and Allison.

One of the policemen took Allison aside. "I know who you are, and Murphy is not going to be happy about this. He doesn't lose his temper much, but when he does, watch out! Good luck with that."

As if by magic, Allison looked up to see both Murphy and Jackson sauntering toward the three women, wearing unhappy expressions. Allison's heart began to pound with trepidation knowing she was in trouble.

The policeman who had been speaking to Allison stepped aside. "Do you want us to take him in, Murphy?"

"You got it. Jackson and I will catch up with him in a bit. Right now, we have our hands full with these three ladies."

Murphy began to usher the women to the bench where Allison had been sitting previously. Jackson had hold of Bella and Marianne's arms, pulling them forward while Murphy held Allison back. "What the hell were you thinking?" he demanded, anger on his face.

"How did you know where to find us?" she asked, confused.

"We received a call from the person we had following you," he responded. "He knew you were in trouble when he saw how much money you were taking out of the bank."

"You had me followed?" she cried.

"I told you that we were going to keep an eye on you for a while to make sure you didn't get in trouble," he stated in a firm tone.

"I still can't believe you had someone following me," she said, trailing after Murphy as he headed to the bench. "I can take care of myself, you know!" she hollered.

He turned to look at Allison and then back at her friends. "I have to admit that the three of you showed us that," he responded. "Now, gather your things, ladies. You're coming with us to the police station. We need you to make your statements," ordered Murphy in a no-nonsense voice.

Marianne and Allison rolled their eyes upon hearing this, and Bella swore. Allison and Marianne went to Bella, hugging her, sympathizing with her dislike of anything to do with the police. Then, Allison grabbed Bella's hand, pulling her forward. "C'mon, let's hurry. I have to use the bathroom … too much coffee this morning."

Chapter 31

Allison climbed the stairs to her apartment, loaded down with Halloween candy. Time seemed to have floated by. She was riding on a cloud with her budding romance with Murphy and her newly revised financial status. Tonight, she'd meet up with her girlfriends at their favorite pub. Life couldn't be better.

As soon as she set her packages down to unlock the door, a figure rushed from behind, grabbing her and wrapping his arms around her. Allison immediately swung the heel of her shoe back into the shin of the man behind her. He hollered, "Ow! What did you do that for?"

Recognizing his voice, she exclaimed, "What the hell, Murphy?"

Looking like a scolded little boy, he replied, "I was happy to see you, that's all."

"Instead, you scared me to death!" Watching Murphy rub his leg, she bit back a smile. When she'd chosen these shoes, she had thought then that they'd make a good weapon. Guess she was right.

"Why are you here, Murphy?" Allison asked.

"I wanted to tell you in person that Susan's file was moved to cold case status. The word on the street is that Susan's death was mafia-related. A retaliation kill. I'm sorry, Allison."

"She's a cold case because of mafia involvement?" she asked, frustrated.

"Basically," he acknowledged. "I'll continue to work the case on my own … when I have the time."

Allison stood in shock, not moving. How was she going to be able to go forward in her life, not knowing why Susan had been murdered? She wanted revenge against those responsible for her death. How was she going to get that?

"Are you okay, Allison?" asked Murphy, concerned.

"No, I'm not! And I won't be until I know who and why Susan was murdered."

"Sometimes, Allison, you just need to let things go; if not, it'll drive you crazy."

Allison knew he was right, but she couldn't leave behind the idea that Susan had been murdered because she was a "fast woman," or a whore as Carlo had called her. She didn't want Susan to be remembered that way. There had been so much speculation and criticism about how Susan had lived her life as a model … mostly from people who'd never met her.

It had even happened last week at the bank where Allison worked. She'd been heading toward the lunchroom when she heard voices ahead but was far enough away not to make out what was said. Coming closer, she overheard one of her co-workers say, "… and you know what goes on with models, don't you? They all bed-hop and end up getting what they deserve as far as I'm concerned."

Allison walked into the employee lunchroom and spotted two women approaching the doorway who looked at her in surprise, wearing guilty looks. Both were in their middle years wearing uninspiring, dull clothing and looked as if they had no life of their own, preferring to infringe and judge the lives of others instead. Allison let her temper get the best of her and, without hesitation, said, "I feel sorry for you both. You know nothing about Susan, and it's sad to see that you have nothing better to do than judge a good, decent person without ever having met her."

The women blushed and, with heads down, made their way around her to leave. After Allison stepped fully into the room, she noticed several women covering their mouths, trying not to laugh out loud. Allison plopped down in one of the chairs surrounding the large, round wooden table and sighed. One woman sitting there began to clap her hands silently. "It's about time someone put those two in their place."

Allison looked at the ladies, "I should never have . . ."

"No need to apologize. As sad as it seems, some people get their high on knocking others down. I'm Loretta, by the way, in customer service."

Meeting Loretta that day turned out to be fortunate, for she was one of the few people who understood Allison's determination to see things to the end by finding out who killed Susan and why. Since they often arranged to meet at lunchtime, she wondered what Loretta would think about this turn of events.

"Allison to earth. What's going on?" Murphy asked, worried. "C'mon, let me help you get these packages inside."

♥ ♥ ♥

Bella was nervous about meeting the noted physician who was visiting. He was instrumental in bringing to the forefront his belief that an additional way of treating cancer patients was through diet. The combination of drugs and diet is what he'd be teaching and demonstrating for the next six weeks at the hospital. Bella was already late for her first training session with him and hoped she could sneak into the room without being noticed. She'd stayed behind to calm a young girl who was missing her mother, who'd gone to the cafeteria for food.

When she arrived at the small conference room, Bella peeked inside the room and saw that it was packed. Searching for an empty seat, Bella could make out only one vacancy … in the front row. Unsure what to do, Bella stood in the doorway, which, much to her horror, caught the speaker's attention. "C'mon in. Don't keep us waiting," he barked.

Although she wished she could turn back, Bella straightened her shoulders and made her way to the front row with flushed cheeks. As soon as she sat down, Bella grabbed her pen and opened her notebook, unaware of the stares she was receiving. Watching her, the doctor remained silent, waiting for Bella to get settled. He turned to the crowd, holding his hand up, and asked, "Is everyone here now?"

Bella was mortified and felt her cheeks warm even more as he turned, looking her way. Noting her discomfort, the doctor suddenly winked at her, something she was sure no one else could see because of the angle of her seat. The doctor continued his speech, and Bella fell into the rhythm of his words, making notes of some of the questions she wanted him to clarify.

A code-blue signal interrupted their session, and Bella immediately slapped her notebook closed and rose to leave. It had to do with one of her patients, and she raced out of the room, hollering over her shoulder, "So sorry, doctor, I've got to go!"

She overheard him ask, "Is she always like this?" and a chuckle rose from the crowd.

At the moment, Bella couldn't worry about anything but the little boy who was at the end of his life. He was one of her favorites, and she would miss his remarkable spirit terribly. She raced by the nursing station and stood outside the door catching her breath and calming herself before entering the boy's room. His parents wore the same expression she'd seen on so many faces at times like this—a begging for a miracle that she couldn't provide. But, as soon as she stood close to the patient, Bella brought a sense of peace to the room, and with her nearby, the patient was better able to let go of life. It was a special gift that she had, and why some whispered she was a "Death Angel."

After taking care of the details that went along with the passing of the little boy, Bella made her way into the doctor's breakroom. She made a fresh pot of coffee and was pouring herself a cup when a voice asked, "Is that for me?"

She turned and stared at the visiting doctor, tongue-tied. The doctor reached his hand forward and gently removed the cup from her hand. "Thank you, Miss …?"

Jolted out of her stupor, she said, "Bella Jones. It's nice to meet you, Dr. Kowasaki."

"Likewise, Dr. Bella Jones. Do you have a few minutes? Sit and tell me about your work here."

Bella looked into his intelligent almond eyes set high on his handsome face and liked what she saw. His Japanese features interested her, and she instinctively knew she'd have to rise to the challenge to meet him on an intellectual basis. Something Bella knew she could do. She felt a flash of disappointment that she wouldn't be able to spend more time with him, but that night, Bella was meeting Allison and Marianne. "I'm sorry, but I have another appointment. Is it possible for a rain check?"

"How about dinner tomorrow night? I hear the food here in Boston is so good that it's difficult to choose which restaurant to go to. What do you suggest?"

"So many are excellent. It just depends upon what you're in the mood for at the time," Bella answered with a smile.

He studied her, intrigued with her lack of fussing over him. He wasn't used to being blown off, especially since he had an abundance of beautiful women who craved his attention. "Okay, give me your telephone number, and I'll call you tomorrow to confirm. Is seven o'clock okay with you?"

Bella nodded and, after giving him her telephone number, she left, wondering what she had gotten herself into. What was she thinking?

♥ ♥ ♥

Marianne didn't answer Jeremy's call. She was trying to step away from him, not wanting to get involved romantically with him. She was falling for him, liking him more and more as time went by. She was no dope. Marianne knew he had other women in his life, and she didn't want to end up with a broken heart.

When the receptionist announced Jeremy's third call, Marianne grunted and answered it. Immediately, he began to plea with her. "Why are you avoiding me?

Is it something I said? We need to talk, Marianne. Can we meet for dinner tonight?"

Marianne sighed into the phone, aware of the people around her, listening to her one-sided conversation as she sat in her open space outside the door of the lawyer she assisted. "I can't meet you tonight; I have plans," she answered in a low voice.

"When, then?"

With curious people looking her way, she wanted to end the call as soon as possible, so she spit out, "Tomorrow night?"

"I think I can arrange that. I'll pick you up at six o'clock. See you then, Marianne," Jeremy said, hanging up, not allowing her a way out.

As Marianne headed to the pub, she'd discuss her dilemma with her friends. She was over her head in dealing with Jeremy and her growing feelings for him. She needed their guidance.

She thought of her aunt and wondered why she had pushed Marianne to consider Jeremy as a life partner—especially if he was after her money. Marianne reviewed what she knew about her aunt as a savvy businesswoman. As a young widow, she had talked the bank into giving her a mortgage on a large house that needed a lot of work completed when she barely had enough money to buy it. At the time, it was unheard of for banks doing such a thing if a man wasn't listed on the mortgage. Yet, her aunt had done just that.

Not a frivolous woman, her aunt was careful with her money. Through time and wise decisions, her investments in the stock market had grown substantially, leaving Marianne a surprising amount of wealth.

Marianne shook her head. So why did her aunt want her to marry Jeremy then? What was it she saw in him that made her determined to bring them together? What did her aunt know that she didn't?

In hindsight, it amazed Marianne to realize how closed off she and her aunt were to express their inner thoughts to each other. How sad. Her aunt had died suddenly without warning, and she wondered if their relationship would have changed in time. Probably not.

Thinking again of Jeremy, Marianne smiled at the thought of how they must have looked at the lobster shack with melted butter dripping from their full mouths of lobster. Jeremy had reached across the table to wipe away a drip of butter from her chin and then had put his finger in his mouth, licking it. That movement had turned her on, and he had noticed her heated cheeks and simply smiled.

With his handsome looks, Jeremy turned many heads his way. Seeing this, Marianne had to remind herself that she was there at his request, and she alone had the power to be with him or not. Curious about her aunt's enthusiasm for her and Jeremy to join forces, Marianne was determined to see him on a deeper level than the superficial one of how he looked. After all, looks faded in time.

Marianne pushed away from her thoughts as she approached the pub. She was looking forward to meeting Bella and Allison.

Chapter 32

Allison was surprised to be the first to arrive at the pub. When Murphy had unexpectantly shown up at her door earlier, he had interfered with her timing, and she thought she wouldn't make it to the pub in time to meet her friends. Smiling at the thought of him, she had liked how he had gathered her in his arms and passionately kissed her in a way her mother wouldn't have approved. Before she reached the stage of no return, she'd pushed away from him. "No, Murphy, I have to meet the girls. I promised them I'd be there."

At his disappointment, she added, "You wouldn't like it if I backed out of plans I'd made with you, right?"

Murphy chuckled. "Right you are, my little minx. Get going then," he ordered, love tapping her behind. "I'll see you tomorrow night."

Allison had studied his cheery face so open with love for her that it made her heart race. Things were getting serious. How was this relationship going to end up?

Once inside the pub, Allison called out, "Hi, Mike! Bella and Marianne will be here shortly, so get those Cosmos started!" she ordered, laughing.

Grinning, Mike held his thumb up in reply. "I saved the table for you."

Once they decided on a date and time to meet, Marianne would call Mike to reserve their favorite booth in the back. And he always made sure it was ready for them with a bowl of nibbles waiting.

Since Halloween was only a few days away, Allison had already seen some teenage mischief-makers dressed in costumes roaming the city streets. Upon seeing them, a chill had run down her back. Ever since she was a kid, Halloween masks scared and intimidated her. They looked so real to her.

Allison settled into the booth and let her shoulders relax. With Christmas not that far away, people were taking out small loans for holiday spending, and it'd kept Allison busy all week.

Alone in the booth, her thoughts turned to Murphy. If anyone asked her if she thought her future included him, she'd have to say it did. She had already slept with him, which she hadn't done lightly. It had seemed so natural to have happened. She had enjoyed the sex they'd shared, but it put a different slant on the relationship in Allison's mind. As much as she thought he was serious about her—or she wouldn't have gone to bed with him— he hadn't said he loved her. That bothered her.

♥ ♥ ♥

Bella rushed along, knowing she had to hurry if she didn't want to be late to meet the girls. When she and the famed doctor had talked, there'd been an energy connection between them. And now, her stomach churned with excitement and nervousness at the idea of having dinner with him the next night. She found him intriguing—someone not afraid to step out with his vision of how food consumption made a difference in health to the point of possibly putting cancer at bay. It made some sense to her. The expression, "You are what you eat," came to mind. But Bella knew there was more to it than that. There had to be a relationship between mind and body for the balance needed to heal. She wondered what the doctor thought about that.

Bella understood herself well enough to know that she was here on earth to help the little ones cross over. A vision of the future crossed her mind, and with it came the understanding that she would never be a mother in the traditional sense but would connect to more children than she could imagine possible. Knowing that made her heart falter for a moment as Bella grasped what that meant. It was a loss of sorts, and yet she'd have so much more.

Her thoughts turned to Dr. Kowasaki. He was quite a bit older than she was. What was it he'd found so interesting about her that he'd invited her to join him for dinner? Bella shook her head in wonderment. She'd know soon enough.

Bella heard footsteps and looked to see Marianne coming her way. Despite the crease of worry on her face, her eyes sparkled, and she wore a glow that Bella hadn't seen before. She reached for Marianne's hand in greeting.

♥ ♥ ♥

Marianne gladly took hold of Bella's hand, and together, they pushed their way through the pub's door, laughing. After waving to Mike, they headed Allison's way. Marianne's heart lifted at being in the company of her friends. God, she loved them so. And she knew she could openly share with them her worries about her relationship with Jeremy.

Allison's cheeks were pink, and Marianne thought it was from more than the chilly air outside. She was glowing, and her eyes were alight with joy. She bet it had to do with Murphy.

"Look at what love can do! You're absolutely glowing, Allison!" exclaimed Marianne.

Allison's cheeks warmed. "I was going to say the same thing about you and Bella both. What's going on with you two?"

Marianne and Bella dumped their coats at the end of the semi-circular booth and squeezed in beside

Allison on the other side. The waitress came to deliver their Cosmos. "Compliments of Mike," she said as she set down a large bowl of nibbles on their table and left.

After they knocked glasses, Allison commanded, "All right, Bella, spill! What's going on with you? I've never seen you like this!"

Bella took a sip of her Cosmo before shyly admitting, "Well, it seems that I have an unexpected date tomorrow night."

"You? A date? Someone who declared that you weren't interested in dating at all?" exclaimed Marianne smiling.

Bella shrugged. "It might be just about business, but..."

"But?" asked Allison in a teasing voice. Then seeing Bella's expression, she added, "You like him, don't you?"

Bella nodded. "There's something about him."

"So, tell! Who is he?"

Bella eagerly told them about meeting Dr. Kowasaki when she'd been late to his class and the conversation they'd had before she'd left the hospital.

"You and the famed, handsome Asian. I like it. You've got to call us immediately after your dinner with him and let us know how it went," ordered Allison with excitement.

Bella and Marianne smiled at Allison's enthusiasm.

"Allison, I think she'll let us know in her own time since she might be too busy to even think about us!" declared Marianne.

Bella's face warmed as she joined in laughing at Allison and Marianne's teasing.

Noting Marianne's glowing face, Allison asked, "So, what's going on with you, Marianne?"

Marianne grimaced. "I'm thinking of ending my involvement with Jeremy."

Bella frowned. "I thought you liked him?"

"That's just it … I do. Maybe more than just a friend, which is the problem."

"Does this have to do with you thinking it's about the money?" asked Allison.

Marianne nodded.

"Then, why don't you ask him?" Allison said.

"What do you mean … ask him?"

"I agree with Allison. You could nicely confront him to see if his interest in you is because his family lost their money and wanted him to marry you for your money," Bella explained.

"No decent Southern woman would dare to ask that," gulped Marianne.

"You're not in the south anymore, Marianne. You deserve to know where he stands if you want to be in any relationship with him," Allison said.

"Allison is right, Marianne. You need to hear it straight from the horse's mouth."

Marianne sat silent, lost in thought. Then, she sat up straighter. "You're both right. I'll work it out somehow."

Bella said, "So, Allison, how are you and Murphy getting along?"

Allison blushed and, for once, seemed out of words.

"Oh, my God! You've done the deed," Bella stated knowingly. "It's written across your face."

Allison turned crimson.

"I hope it was as good as your expression says it was," Bella laughed, causing the others to join in.

When she caught her breath, Allison admitted, "It was and so much more. It's just … just…"

"Just what?" asked Marianne.

"I think Murphy loves me by the way he behaves around me, but he hasn't said so in words," Allison said miserably.

Bella said, "We are our mother's child, aren't we?"

"What do you mean?" Allison asked.

"We were taught to think that if a boy likes us, that was enough, right? But we got lost in the shuffle of what we thought about the boy. In other words, it was always one-sided whether the boy was happy, leaving us obligated to make him so. It was never about if we were happy in the relationship. And, more so, we weren't taught to ask for what we wanted in the relationship to make us happy."

"That's true. And if God forbid, we had sex with the boy, he needed to marry us because we were considered spoiled goods. At least, that's what my catholic upbringing dictated," confessed Allison.

"And sex changes the dynamics of the relationship. It tightens our hold on the guy and loses its ease. At least it did for me the two times I had sex with a guy. I demanded more of him than I would have of any girlfriend—if I would have had one," admitted Marianne.

"Thank God, these are the 1980s, and time has changed some things. So, let's get back to basics. How do you honestly feel about Murphy, Allison?" asked Bella. "What do you want from the relationship?"

Allison was quiet. After a few minutes, she looked at her friends and her eyes filled. "I want him to love me more each day. I want to always see the love shining from his eyes, knowing I'm the cause of it. I want him to want me as much as I do him. I want to grow old together. And I want to give him enough of my heart to love him unconditionally, yet, be able to share the rest of my heart with the people I love … like you."

Bella and Marianne blinked their surprise at her deep-felt tenderness. Immediately, they grabbed onto Allison's hands and said in one voice, "Amen."

Chapter 33

The following night, Allison was looking forward to seeing Murphy. They were dining at the high-end restaurant, Samuels, on Boston's waterfront—something Allison had requested to do. She'd heard one of the women at the bank rave about how splendid the restaurant had been before its renovation, and it was supposed to be even better now. Typically, she preferred a more casual environment, but she liked the idea of getting dressed up for a change.

Allison dressed carefully and tied her hair back, letting it fall straight down her back. She opened a new mascara and liberally applied it, making her eyes stand out. With the few pounds she'd lost since Susan's death, her cheekbones were more prominent, chiseling her features even more. Allison smiled when she stood back and viewed herself in the mirror. She liked what she saw and felt flirty in her new sleeveless black dress.

When the doorbell rang, she hurried to let Murphy in. To her surprise, it was not Murphy standing there but Jackson.

"Hi, Jackson! What are you doing here?" She blushed at her rudeness. "That didn't sound right. I'm glad to see you … just surprised."

Jackson's large eyes looked troubled.

Panic began to fill Allison. "What is it? What's wrong?"

"Murphy's been hurt. Come with me, and I'll take you to him," he urged.

"What happened?" she choked out. "Is Murphy okay?"

"We'll know shortly. He was shot in the chest when we disrupted a holdup. He's in surgery to remove the bullet. I've got the patrol car waiting outside. Better grab a jacket; it's cold outside."

"Oh, my God! Murphy's going to make it, isn't he?"

"He's strong. We just have to trust he'll pull through," encouraged Jackson.

Allison's heart dropped. This was a nightmare! After what'd happened to Susan, she wasn't sure she could survive if Murphy didn't make it. She couldn't lose him … she just couldn't. She grabbed her coat and purse and locked her door. Jackson had gone ahead, and she was out of breath by the time she caught up with him.

"Where are we going? Which hospital?" Allison asked as they swung out into the traffic.

"Brigham and Women's."

Allison brightened. Brigham and Women's Faulkner Hospital in Jamaica Plains was what she liked best. "Was Murphy conscious after he was shot?" she asked.

"He asked for you, Allison."

As Allison's eyes filled, Jackson rested his hand on hers for a moment. "I'm so sorry, Allison. I didn't see the guy in time to stop him."

She shrugged. "It's not your fault, Jackson. You can't plan how things are going to work out in a job like yours."

Jackson pulled into the emergency room entranceway and parked the car. They both jumped out and raced inside. Jackson approached the desk and asked about Murphy. After speaking with the desk clerk, he waved his hand at Allison to follow him.

Sitting in the waiting room, nervously tapping her foot, Allison wondered how many times she'd be doing this very thing if she and Murphy were to marry. A cop's life wasn't for the weak—for the cop or the life partner. She would have to trust the Universe that all was as it was supposed to be. Could she do that? *Don't get ahead of yourself, Allison,* she scolded herself.

♥ ♥ ♥

Bella was nervous, feeling like a scared teenager going in front of the principal as she waited inside the restaurant for Dr. Kowasaki to arrive. They had decided it would be easier for them to meet at the restaurant than for him to pick her up miles out of his way.

As soon as she arrived, she was ushered to a corner table. The doctor had made the reservations and had alerted the restaurant to expect her. Settling in, she looked up to see him approach—a handsome man with gray at his temples and an easy way of moving forward with a smile. He looked delighted to see her already there, waiting for him. Bella's heart raced as he got closer. There was something about him that tugged at her heart.

"Hello, my dear. I'm so glad to see you," he said.

"And I to see you, Dr. Kowasaki," Bella replied with a smile.

"Please, no formality tonight. Call me James," he said as he bent and lifted her hand to his mouth, kissing it lightly.

James sat across from her and looked around. "This is very attractive. I like all the woodwork and lighting. A very nice choice, my dear."

"I'm glad you like it. I think you're going to be pleased with the excellent food choices they offer as well."

"I'm sure I will, but it doesn't matter as long as I spend time with you," he stated gallantly.

At first, Bella was put off by his words. She wasn't used to anyone sounding so glib, but as she studied him, he seemed to mean what he'd said. He continued, "I'm always so busy that it's not very often that I get to spend time with a beautiful woman. I've decided that my life is passing by without some of the wonderful things it has to offer me." He smiled. "I can see by your expression that you are wondering if I'm being sincere or just blowing you smoke as some of you younger ones say," he added, smiling.

Bella blushed and chuckled.

The waiter came. "Sir, are you ready for the bottle of wine you ordered?"

James nodded. "Please."

Bella cocked her head. "You ordered wine for us?"

"The very best Pinot Noir they had. I hope that is okay with you?"

"I love a good red wine," she answered.

"Good. I think you'll like this one. I first had it when I was in California a few years back, and I always search for it wherever I stay."

"Do you travel a lot?" Bella asked.

"Too much, which is why I decided to stay put for the next six weeks and see how I adjust to being in one spot for a while. I'm serious about wanting to enjoy life with a slower pace."

"Boston is the perfect spot to try that out. There's so much history and cultural happenings where you can do as much or as little as you want."

James reached for her hand. "I don't mean to scare you, Bella, but I'd like to do that with you. I want to get to know you better. I think that we have a special connection, and I'd like to explore that."

Bella thought of removing her hand but didn't want to hurt his feelings. James seemed to sense that and tightened his grip. Bella raised her eyes to his and felt a flash of energy, causing her feminine parts to awaken, confirming what the doctor had said.

"We'll take one day at a time, okay?" James asked.

Bella nodded as the waiter came with the bottle of wine for them to share.

♥ ♥ ♥

Marianne marched her way to the door to let Jeremy in. She needed to remain strong if she was going to find out if he was interested in her or her money. Marianne dreaded confrontation, and she wanted their conversation to be as smooth and kind as she could make it. She had set out wine and some appetizers to sit and talk, deciding if they would continue seeing each other.

Sophie was delighted to see Jeremy and danced at his feet as he stepped inside. He swooped down and lifted the dog into his arms, where he received many kisses for his effort. Despite her resolve to be all business, Marianne smiled at the two of them. Jeremy leaned forward, dog in hand, to kiss Marianne on the cheek.

"Come on inside. I have a glass of wine waiting and some appetizers. I want to talk to you about something," she said.

"This sounds serious," Jeremy said as he followed behind her into the kitchen.

Marianne remained quiet as she poured the wine and handed Jeremy his glass. He sniffed it and took a small sip rolling it around in his mouth. He smiled. "This is good. Is it a California wine?"

She nodded.

"So, what do you want to talk about?" Jeremy asked as he reached for a cracker with brie.

Marianne closed her eyes to gather her strength. "I want to know why you are interested in dating me. I know that your family lost its money and that your granny and my aunt wanted us to get married. Is it about my money?"

Jeremy's face turned beet red. Then, he burst out laughing. "Is that what you think? It's about your money?"

It was Marianne's turn to blush. "Well? Isn't it?"

"My dear Marianne, a few years back, when I was a new stockbroker, I asked my granny if I could invest some of her money for her. She signed over a hefty sum for me to invest. I invested it in a stock that went south for a while. I couldn't get her to understand that the stock would regain its worth in time, and I'd be able to reinvest it in something else, which I did. I bought Microsoft stock when it was low, making her a small fortune. However, because of the one stock that lost a little money, Granny will always think I lost the family's fortune, and I've given up trying to convince her otherwise. As a stockbroker, I make an excellent living, and I have no interest in your money unless you'd like me to invest it for you."

Marianne looked uncertain. "Ohh."

"Marianne, I'm an intelligent man, and when my granny and your aunt wanted us to get together and marry, I thought you must be a poor, pathetic thing who couldn't get a man on your own. And growing up, the few times I visited my granny, you were never around; you were away at school. To be honest, I wasn't interested in meeting you at all."

"So, what changed your mind?" asked Marianne with burning cheeks.

"I saw your picture in the newspaper with your friends. You know what article I'm talking about. I liked what I saw and thought I'd give you a call."

"You called me a few times before then. Why?"

"Duty. I promised my granny I would … that's all."

"Ohh."

Jeremy set his glass down and came to her side. He gathered her in his arms and kissed her thoroughly on the mouth. "I don't know why you are so concerned with why I'm interested in you, but I find you a very desirable, headstrong woman whom I'd like to get to know better. Would you allow me to do that, my princess?"

"I guess so," she said with a smile, leaning in for another kiss.

Chapter 34

Finally, Allison was allowed to see Murphy. When she walked through the hospital door and saw Murphy lying there with tubes attached to his body and the heart monitor beeping, she burst into tears. She sat beside his bed and held his limp hand in hers. He looked so helpless lying there—like a big teddy bear with the wind knocked out of him.

It had been a long night for both of them. Allison tightened her grip, not wanting to lose contact with him. When she felt a weak response from him, she immediately rose from her chair and leaned over him. "Murphy? I'm right here. Can you hear me?"

He blinked several times and slowly opened one eye. Seeing Allison there, Murphy gave a weak smile. "Hi there, sweetheart," he said in a hoarse voice.

Allison bent to kiss him. Jackson came through the door and stood by the bed next to her as she did. "Hey, man, you had us worried there for a moment. Glad to see you've joined the living."

"Yeah, that's what happens when you've got a beautiful girl to return to," he croaked, looking at Allison.

"Here, drink some of this water, Murphy," urged Allison.

"The doctor says that you're going to be okay after a few days' rest. Can I get you anything?" Jackson asked.

"Yeah, the hide of the guy who shot me."

"Already happened. He tried to escape, and we got him."

Allison listened to Murphy and Jackson talk about the robber being dead, and goosebumps covered her body. Is that what happens—a person's life becomes just a body when a bullet hits its mark?

Jackson stepped closer and placed his hand on Murphy's shoulder. "I'm heading home to change my clothes and then to the precinct to fill out the paperwork. I'm glad to see you doing okay, buddy."

"Yeah, me too. See you later," Murphy said.

After Jackson left, Murphy turned to Allison, taking in her fancy dress. "You've been here all night?"

"Well, I wasn't going to go anywhere until I knew you were okay," she said, admonishing him with a smile. "Some of your family is waiting to see you, so I'm going to go home and leave you in their hands. I need to get some rest since tomorrow is a workday for me."

"Thank you, Allison, for being by my side all night. I'm glad you were here for me."

"Of course, Murphy. Why wouldn't I be?"

"I just want you to know…."

"Yes, he's awake!" Murphy's mother announced to others behind her. I hope that I'm not interrupting anything," she questioned, looking between the two.

Murphy groaned and then winked at Allison. His mother patted Allison on the back. "You better get some rest now, honey. We'll take over." Surprising Murphy, his mother leaned into Allison and kissed her cheek. "Thank you for everything."

Allison left the room, feeling warm inside. She liked Murphy's mother, and the thought that they might share Murphy's love wasn't a bad thing at all.

♥ ♥ ♥

Bella woke with a slight headache. She wasn't used to drinking as much wine as she had last night. She leaned back in bed, thinking about the doctor and how attuned to her thoughts he seemed to be. Unlike most men she'd been with, James devoured her words and ideas, demanding more from her. Bella had shared with him some she'd never spoken out loud. He was tender with her, sensing she was uncertain about his fascination with her. Perhaps it was his being from a different culture and older than she was, but she loved his sureness in what he wanted from her. And there was a part of her that wanted to give herself to him in ways she had yet to give to another soul.

When her telephone rang, she half-expected it to be James only to have Allison on the other end. "Good morning, Bella!"

"Hi, Allison! This is a surprise. What's happening?"

Learning about Allison's unsettling night, Bella was sorry that Murphy had been shot but was glad to know he would be okay. If Allison and Murphy did decide to marry, Bella thought that a phone call like this wouldn't be the last one. Bella tried to find the right words to comfort Allison. "Are you okay, Allison?"

"Yes, I just wanted to share what happened last night and, more to the point, find out how your date with the famed doctor went."

Bella felt her face warm. "You know, I really like him. He's a great guy, and we talked for hours. He's testing the waters of staying in one place for more than a week or two at a time and has asked me to acquaint him with Boston."

"And, of course, you said yes ...?"

Bella laughed. "Yes, I did. It'll be fun seeing Boston through his eyes."

"And does that include you showing him more than Boston if you know what I mean?" Allison asked bluntly in a teasing manner.

"You never know," answered Bella with a shiver of pleasure at the thought.

♥ ♥ ♥

Marianne felt Sophie beside her as she opened one eye to the world. Having sensed her movement, Sophie stood over Marianne and kissed her awake. "Ooh, stop, Sophie! Come here, little girl!" she said, laughing and clutching the dog into her arms.

After petting and calming the dog, Marianne thought of the conversation between Jeremy and herself. She was pleased to know the truth about his financial situation and thought how much better it was to have asked him about it than to avoid asking, no matter how embarrassing it was.

Her bedside phone rang, and thinking it might be Jeremy, Marianne answered it, about to say hello. But instead, she was surprised to hear Allison's voice. "Good morning, Sunshine. How goes it?"

Marianne laughed. "Well, good morning, Sunshine, to you! How was your date with Murphy last night?"

Allison's voice got subdued. "Not what I had expected, that's for sure."

"Spill. What happened?" Marianne asked, worried.

Allison caught her up to date on what had happened to Murphy, then asked Marianne, "How about you? Did you and Jeremy straighten things out?"

Sounding pleased, Marianne told Allison about her conversation with Jeremy.

"You must be happy about that," Allison said.

"Yes, although it doesn't solve everything. As you know, Jeremy has dated many women and hasn't stayed with any one of them for any length of time. I might be just another one he loses interest in."

"So, what are you going to do?" Allison asked. "Just give up?"

"Well, no, but I'm not going to jump right into bed with him, either!"

Hearing what she'd said and knowing Allison had done just that, Marianne sucked in her breath and fumbled for the right words to say. "...Not that there's anything wrong with it, but I don't want to change our relationship until I can be sure that I'm not just a fling for him."

"You'll know in time. Just trust your gut," assured Allison.

After ending their conversation, Marianne reflected on her feelings for Jeremy. There was no denying it—she was falling for him. And the thought of going to bed with him made her insides flutter with anticipation despite telling Allison she wouldn't do that. She hoped she was strong enough to be true to her words.

1984

Chapter 35

One Year Later

Allison waddled her way into the bar where Marianne and Bella waited for her. Being pregnant with twins wasn't easy, especially since they were due in a few weeks.

When she'd first discovered she was pregnant, she had cried ... not at the idea of being pregnant. It was more than that. As much as Allison knew that Murphy loved her, he still hadn't said so in words. And she had stubbornly made up her mind that she wasn't going to tell him about the baby until he said he loved her. Marianne and Bella had argued against her doing that, but she had remained firm until the moment it had all become undone. That had happened when Allison had gone to the grocery store and had run into Murphy's mother.

Allison and Murphy's mother had become close ever since Murphy's time in the hospital. Each time there was a family gathering, the two sought each other out, enjoying the company of the other. Murphy's family was large and noisy, with no daughter and so many boys of all ages wrestling each other and joking around that it was in constant upheaval. Murphy's mother had her hands full, but it was clear she adored them all, especially her husband. Allison loved joining Murphy when he visited his family. She felt at home there and was doted upon as the daughter his parents had never had.

Meeting Murphy's mother that day, Allison had felt exposed, thinking anyone who saw her would know she was pregnant. When Murphy's mother asked how she was, Allison tried not to look her in the eye when she answered a simple "Okay."

Studying Allison, Murphy's mother had put her arm around her and pulled her aside. "Does Murphy know?"

Allison had burst into tears and shook her head, clutching onto the older woman's shoulder. "Please, don't tell him."

"Why haven't you said anything to him?"

Allison's face turned crimson.

"You can tell me, Allison. I won't say a word to him about what we discuss. I promise."

"It's just that Murphy has never told me that he loves me."

"Of course, he loves you, Allison! I see it every time he looks at you," Murphy's mother said, bewildered

"But he has never said so. I know I must sound like a silly teenager, but I believe that until someone can say I love you in words, it's not so." Allison shook her head. "At least that has been my experience. I don't know if you can understand what I'm trying to say."

"I think I can. I'm just surprised that my big lug of a son hasn't said this to you since he has told his father and me how much he loves you. I've never seen my son so happy, Allison." She paused. "Have you told Murphy how much you love him?"

Surprised at her question, Allison's cheeks reddened. "I wanted to hear it from him first," she confessed.

Murphy's mother smiled. "I don't know who hurt you before, but you're safe with Murphy. He's the type of man who will love you forever—and he will love the baby you've created together. Trust me on this."

Allison wiped tears away, looking embarrassed. "Lately, I find myself crying at the drop of a hat."

Murphy's mother squeezed Allison close. "That's because you're pregnant, my dear," she said, kissing her on the cheek. "I believe we should start planning a wedding…what do you think?"

♥ ♥ ♥

Bella was happy to find the time to meet with her friends. She and her now-husband were back in town after traveling the globe working with other doctors and nurses throughout the health community, promoting better dietary and meditation practices.

Bella had been surprised at how easily her relationship with James had developed into a loving and sexually satisfying one, causing her to accept his marriage proposal. When James had told her beforehand that there was no possibility of having children naturally with him, Bella remembered her vision of sensing that she wouldn't be a mother in the traditional sense. Not to be deterred from working with children, part of her agreement to join James as his partner in the medical field was for her to have the opportunity to be with the children wherever they traveled. She came alive when she spent time with them, allowing her to comfort them, showing them love and ways to cope with their illnesses. And her reputation as the "Death Angel" followed her wherever they went.

The more she traveled with James, the more her world opened for her to see how fortunate Americans were to have so many possibilities to live the way they wanted. The saddest part of this new work for Bella was to see children starving. So many people worldwide were barely surviving, scratching out their living with little food available and limited materials to protect and keep them safe. Bella was humbled each time she received a thank you for her help.

Upon finding Bella weeping one day, James had asked her if their work was too much for her. She had smiled through her tears and answered, "It is what gives me life ... precious life."

James had stilled at her words and studied her with smoldering eyes. Saying nothing, he'd led her into the bedroom, where he silently undressed her and made endless love to her. "You are my life," he whispered to Bella as she lay in his arms, and she had never been happier.

♥ ♥ ♥

Marianne hurried along to reach the bar in time. So much had happened this past year for all of them. Allison was pregnant with twins—boys! Bella was now a world traveler with her new husband, James, and here she was about to marry Jeremy.

Marianne had asked her friends to meet her at the bar in memory of all the times they had shared there. It was unlikely that there would be many more occasions to repeat it since Bella traveled extensively, Allison had moved to "Southie," and she would be moving back to Atlanta.

Unlike the other two, Marianne had chosen to have a high-end wedding, albeit a small one, and had asked Bella and Allison to be her matrons of honor. Most of the guests would be friends of Jeremy, and she was okay with that. Marianne smiled, remembering how he had surprised her at the Boston Red Sox game by proposing on screen. She had been mortified by all the attention they received but had gamely grinned and nodded yes for all to see. Jeremy had teased her about it, saying it was the only way to ensure she'd say yes to his proposal. Marianne had to agree. She'd put him off twice before, saying they hadn't known each other long enough, but Jeremy had put his foot down, and she was glad he had.

Marianne had set her wedding plans around Bella and Allison's schedule because she wanted—needed—her friends to be with her on her special day. God! She loved them so much. The day they had met in the waiting room had been one of the best days of her life, and nothing could change that.

2017

Chapter 36

34 Years Later

Allison didn't enjoy flying. Each time the plane began its run to lift into the air, she felt the loss of connection to the loved ones she was leaving behind. She closed her eyes tight, holding in the tears that threatened to flow. She straightened and gripped the armrests of her narrow seat, calming her racing heart.

Allison felt the woman next to her as she leaned her way. "Are you okay?"

"I will be after we get airborne," Allison mumbled, embarrassed.

"Where are you headed?" the woman asked.

Aware that the lady was trying to get Allison's mind off her fear of flying, she responded, "I'm headed to Atlanta to meet my two best friends. We haven't had many chances to get together without a specific reason these last 20 plus years, and I'm looking forward to it."

"That sounds wonderful. You're wise to make time to get together before life gets in the way and it's too late."

"Yes, that's what we thought too."

"Are you planning anything special?"

Allison's heart squeezed. "I've asked my friends to join me at a rally taking place in Atlanta. It's a part of the Me Too Movement, and we're attending in memory of my former roommate."

"How interesting," replied the woman. "Well, I wish you all the best."

"Thank you. If you don't mind, I'm going to close my eyes and try to doze. I didn't sleep that well last night. Thanks for helping me through takeoff."

"You're welcome, my dear."

It seemed as if it were only minutes later when the woman next to Allison gently shook her shoulder. "We're getting ready to land."

Allison's cheeks warmed as she realized she had been fully asleep with her mouth hanging open, drool down her chin, and most likely snoring. Not her best look.

Making her way down the aisle, Allison was eager to enjoy the warmer weather that Atlanta offered this time of year. Inside the airport, she searched for signage to take her to the baggage area and the driver waiting for her that Marianne had ordered. They would head to Alpharetta, where Marianne lived.

A handsome young man stepped from the crowd at the bottom of the stairs leading into the baggage area. "Miss Allison, I'm here to drive you home."

"How did you recognize me?"

He laughed. "I couldn't miss you. My mother has pictures of you and Miss Bella all over the house."

Allison chuckled. "Andrew, I have to be honest. You've grown so much that I didn't recognize you at first. I bet you haven't heard anyone say that to you in a long time, especially since you are now married and a father."

Andrew smiled indulgently. "You're right about that. Come this way. Your baggage is unloading on carrousel number 10."

♥ ♥ ♥

Bella's plane was late to arrive in Atlanta. Standing at the Pick-Up curb, she swore she could already feel the difference between California, where she now lived, and the more stuffy, glib atmosphere of the South. Things were so much more relaxed on the west coast.

A limo pulled up to the curb, and a man dressed formally as a chauffeur got out and headed to the rear of the car. "Miz Bella, I'm William. Miz Marianne asked me to pick you up and drive you to Alpharetta. She said to tell you she'll be waiting up for you when you arrive."

"How nice. Thank you, William."

"You've picked an excellent time to visit. The weather has been beautiful this early fall."

She smiled and nodded before stepping into the limo's back seat through the door that William held open.

"Miz Marianne sent you a Cosmo to sip while I drive you there. Here, let me pour it in this special glass so that it won't spill all over you if I have to stop suddenly."

When William handed her the glass, she chuckled. "I can just imagine what Marianne has planned for us and the trouble we are going to get into this time. We're here just for fun—no deaths, weddings, or babies—just fun and relaxation."

"Yes, M'am. That sounds nice. Buckle up, and let's get you there."

Bella leaned back in the seat, the drink in her hand. Her first sip of the Cosmo brought memories of meeting Allison and Marianne for the first time. She smiled to think how having a mammogram the same day had led the three of them to become best friends. Thinking of that, the thought that she should make an appointment for one flashed in her mind. But then she remembered the doctor had said that women her age didn't need to have one unless there was an issue.

Bella was tired and felt each of the 66 years she'd lived. She took two healthy sips of her drink and then put the glass into the holder in the open bar in front of her. Leaning back once more, she closed her eyes and rested. Working with James, Bella had learned how to take short catnaps that would hold her in good stead while they worked their long hours before she could get complete rest.

♥ ♥ ♥

Marianne was excited to have her friends visit. She'd been surprised when Allison had called her about the Me Too Movement rally going on in Atlanta. Eagerly, she had invited her friends to stay with her for an extended length of time since each was free to do so. At this point in their lives, no one had been spared the usual ups and downs of living, and spending time together was something they'd expressed that they needed. Marianne decided she would cherish every moment, particularly in light of what was going on in her life.

When Allison walked through the door with her son, Marianne's spirit lifted. Allison was still so casual and down to earth that she left the impression everyone should shed her shoes, tuck her feet under her, and relax back on the couch. In comparison, Marianne realized she'd once more built a shell around herself during the years of her deteriorating marriage. Now that her divorce was final, she felt she'd be able to celebrate her new life with her best friends.

"I'm so glad to see you, my dear friend," Marianne said before taking her into her arms and holding her tight. She turned to her son, "Thank you, Andrew, for making the trip."

"My pleasure, Mother. I've taken Miss Allison's bags to her room. Do you have everything you need before I take off?"

"All but Bella, whose flight has been delayed. I've hired a limo to pick her up so you can be home with your family."

Marianne was proud of her son as he kissed Allison goodnight before approaching her. He was a good boy, concerned about her. "Goodnight, Sweetheart. I love you and kisses to Rosalie and Isabella," she said.

After settling into the family room, Marianne handed Allison a Cosmo. It was still Marianne's favorite cocktail, and she'd become an expert at making them.

"Hmm … even better than the ones in Boston. Yours are the best Cosmos ever, Marianne," proclaimed Allison. "Did you add a touch of mint?"

"Ahh. You've found my secret," Marianne answered. "A tiny touch is all."

Lost in their own thoughts, Marianne and Allison felt a peace overcome them. Directing her attention to the outside, Allison remarked, "Your garden is so beautiful, Marianne. You truly have a green thumb. It looks so different than the last time I was here. What did you do?"

Delighted that Allison had noticed, Marianne said, "I've been bringing more of the outside in and vice versa … blending the two."

"Well, it's working. It's gorgeous."

They heard gravel crunch and realized that Bella's limo had arrived. Marianne and Allison set down their drinks and hurried to the front door. Stepping outside, they moved forward to envelop Bella in hugs. The three wrapped their arms around each other and hopped up and down, laughing. The limo driver watched them and smiled.

Now that Bella was here, their visit could begin in earnest.

Chapter 37

Allison woke, feeling a bit fuzzy. As she looked around, it came to her that she was in one of Marianne's guestrooms in Atlanta—and probably had too much to drink the night before. She thought back to the first time she'd stayed in one of Marianne's guestrooms in Boston when Susan had been murdered. It was hard to believe that it had been more than 34 years ago.

Allison heard her cell phone ring, sounding muffled. She pinpointed it as coming from her purse resting on the bureau. She got up and made her way there. Looking at the screen, she smiled. "Good morning!"

Allison listened intently, and her eyes lit up with pleasure. "Thank you for checking on me. Yes, I'll tell them. I miss you too, Jackson."

Her friends knew that Jackson had been there for Allison ever since Murphy was killed in a drug raid, leaving her with two sets of twins (all boys) to raise by herself. And thank God, he had. It had been Jackson who had become the boys' father, spending as much time with them as any good father would, much to the annoyance of his now two ex-wives.

At the time, Allison didn't think it was possible to be so devastated and survive the death of her beloved husband. She and the boys had accepted Jackson as their father's friend when he'd first stepped into their lives. At different times throughout the years, she'd caught Jackson looking at her with tenderness and something more. She had pushed it aside, not even considering an intimate relationship with him, handsome as he was. Even if she wanted it, a black man and Irish woman surviving in Southie? Not likely.

However, Jackson had earned respect from the close-knit family and community throughout the years by demonstrating that he was a good man and a true friend to his ex-partner by looking after Allison and the boys. He'd promised Murphy, and he'd done just that, facing off with his five brothers who thought they should be the ones to step in. Jackson had simply stated that he had been the one chosen by Murphy, and that was that.

Only recently, now that the children were grown, Allison looked at Jackson as possibly more than a friend. They had laughed and shared enough times to become comfortable with each other, and it seemed to bond them like many happy couples.

She would never remarry, she'd assured her mother-in-law shortly after Murphy's death. However, toward the end of her life, without words defining Allison's growing relationship with Jackson, they both understood that Jackson was a worthy man and deserved to be loved.

♥ ♥ ♥

Bella had tossed and turned all night. She felt so alive after visiting with her two best friends the night before that she had found it difficult to sleep. She hadn't realized how much she'd missed Marianne and Allison. Aware that each was now at a "certain age" and beginning a new phase of living, Bella had so much she wanted to discuss with them.

Bella thought of Allison. She was aware that she and Jackson had become close over the years, working together to raise four adorable but rambunctious boys who needed a firm hand. Jackson was perfect for the job and doted over them as if he were their father. She believed that Jackson's efforts to do so were part of why he'd failed in both his short-lived marriages. Of course, just being a cop was difficult for any marriage to survive.

Marianne looked the best Bella had seen her in years. There was a glow and ease about Marianne now, and Bella knew it was due to the freedom of pretending that all was okay in her life with Jeremy.

Now free to be her own person, she no longer had to care how her looks or actions might affect Jeremy's business.

Bella drew in a deep breath. Out of the three of them, she thought that she'd had the happiest marriage. Not a day went by that she didn't feel the loss of James not being in her life. It had been fascinating to see him at work, spending endless hours to comfort others. And she missed how later he'd turned into a magnificent lover, never wanting to be parted, leaving them entwined at the end of their lovemaking, always wanting more. Now, her bed was empty … as empty as her heart without him. She told their 28-year-old daughter—adopted from Viet Nam at the age of three—that she didn't think anyone could measure up to James for her to consider being in a relationship with him. Her daughter had patted her shoulder in consolation, causing Bella to smile at the reversal of roles.

♥ ♥ ♥

Marianne was satisfied that neither of her friends suspected that she was waiting to learn if her cancer had returned. Her doctor hadn't liked what he saw on her mammogram, and she'd had a biopsy a week earlier. She was still waiting to hear the verdict, which was a good sign, she thought. Just by having her friends near her, Marianne felt stronger in all ways.

Marianne hadn't realized how relieved she was to be out of her marriage with Jeremy until she had the signed divorce papers in hand. At the beginning of their marriage, they had been very happy together, enjoying each other's company, and thrilled over the birth of their son, Andrew. But like some men from an established family with considerable wealth, Jeremy had lost some of his drive that had existed in Boston. He settled into some ways of the "gentlemen of the south" before him by conducting his business at the country club or on the golf course … always with a cocktail in hand.

Marianne had to admit that Jeremy could be a charmer all right—charming his way into several of her supposed girlfriends' beds. She acknowledged that the more boisterous and loud he became, the quieter she became. That made it easy for Jeremy to point out on a few occasions that it was her cold behavior that'd cost him a potential client. He wasn't willing to look at his own behavior.

The funny thing was that she still loved Jeremy. Though relieved to be divorced, she wished him no harm. Instead, Marianne hoped that he would get help with his drinking problem and turn back into the once lovable man he'd been. Chances were slim for that to happen, but there was always hope. She sighed.

She thought of her granddaughter. At seven years of age, Isabella had captured Marianne's heart and had given her the best reason to be healthy. She didn't want to miss any stage of her life … God willing.

Both Bella and Allison looked beautiful and happy, although she was reminded that they had all aged when she looked at them. She realized all three of them were once again in the waiting room—but this time in the waiting room of life—God's waiting room.

Chapter 38

When Allison padded her way downstairs, she surprised Marianne, already outside on the patio sipping coffee. Allison didn't miss the worry lines on Marianne's face that disappeared as soon as she saw Allison. "Good morning, Marianne."

"Good morning, sweetie. Sit and let me get you a cup of coffee," urged Marianne.

It came to Allison how unusual it was for someone to wait on her. She was the one always waiting on others. Allison plopped down into a chair and leaned back, breathing in the scented air of the garden. After being handed her mug of coffee, Allison bent to inhale the aroma of the coffee. "Hmm. This is exactly what I needed. Thank you, Marianne."

"You're welcome, my friend. I'm so happy that you and Bella are here, and I'm glad you suggested attending the rally. I think it's the right thing to do."

"What's the right thing to do?" asked Bella, joining them, coffee in hand.

"Attending the Me Too Movement rally. You've never gotten closure on Susan's death, have you, Allison?" asked Marianne.

"You know, I think about Susan nearly every day. Because of her, I was able to school my boys and allow them to choose what they wanted to do with their lives."

"Yes, you certainly were fortunate that way. I'm glad for you," Marianne agreed.

"How time flies. It doesn't seem possible that all your boys are full-grown now." Bella said.

Allison chuckled. "You mean possible to have made it to this age without killing each other, don't you?"

Marianne and Bella laughed. Allison's boys were still a hand full, boys being boys, always teasing each other.

"What are your boys doing now, Allison?" Bella asked.

"Well, Erik is a fireman; Philip is a cop; Danny works in IT at Amazon, and Jack is a high school English teacher at the same school they all attended."

"Do you get to see them much?" Marianne asked.

Allison laughed. "Too much, I'm afraid. I swear there's something about Irish boys who don't want to move out and leave their mothers. All but Danny still lives at the house in Southie."

"Any marriages in the works for any of them?" asked Marianne.

"Not so far. Danny has a serious girlfriend whom I like very much. I think they're planning on moving in together." At Bella and Marianne's expressions, Allison laughed. "Not in my house!"

They laughed together, cheered by Allison's hectic but happy life. "The other boys date but aren't serious enough with anyone to think of marrying, at least for now," Allison added.

"How about your daughter Cam, Bella? Is she dating anyone seriously?" asked Marianne.

"No, she's too busy studying and following in her father's footsteps. She reminds me of myself at her age ... all work and no play. I don't know if she will ever marry."

"Things are not like they used to be. Not that long ago, women were expected to marry. Do you remember when I first started dating Murphy what we talked about? I'll never forget you saying, Bella, that we are our mother's child. Remember that?" asked Allison.

Both Bella and Marianne nodded.

"Now girls are free to do what they want. Things sure are different today, and I'm not so sure I like the changes," Allison admitted. "Except maybe for the Me Too Movement. It's about time men take responsibility for their actions."

Bella became lost in her thoughts. "I used to wonder why men think they are entitled to mount any woman they wanted. It took me reading the book 'The Clan of the Cave Bear' to understand the ways of some of Mother Nature's creatures who only understand their role to procreate. In the book, the male bears immediately satisfy their sexual urge without thought of anything more than that. It didn't matter who their partner was, either. I found myself thinking that man has not progressed much further." Bella looked at the others staring at her. "What?"

"What you said certainly pares things down to the nitty-gritty of sex, but I'm distressed to think that men feel it's their right to have sex with any woman there for the taking," stated Marianne.

"Me, too," Allison added.

"I couldn't agree more," replied Bella. "That's why we have to strive to be more than the bears of the book. And I agree with you both that the Me Too Movement is one positive way to take a stance. That's why I'm here ... one of the reasons I'm here with you today. I needed to see my two best friends who I've missed."

Bella could see that Marianne and Allison had been affected by her words. They were thoughtful. Traveling worldwide, Bella was exposed to countless women in nearly every country she visited who had been sexually abused. Dealing with them as a doctor had hardened her to be clinical about it, forgetting that others wouldn't be comfortable with her take on it.

The rally for the Me Too Movement was something that Bella was looking forward to attending. She would be there to support in spirit all those women she'd met in her travels, but the one she'd walk for would be her daughter. When she and Jeremy had come across her, alone on the streets in Hanoi, they were never sure of all that she'd endured. Even to this day, Cam was skittish around men.

Marianne admired Bella and all her knowledge and experience. Bella knew people in ways that she never would. Simply by living around Atlanta, Marianne was sheltered by the old Southern ways of not exposing oneself to the horrible and ugly—that was kept to the privacy of the home.

Having lived in Boston for those years, Marianne had not taken for granted the differences between decent and poor schools according to race—like it was in the south. As soon as she and Jeremy had moved back to Atlanta, Marianne had volunteered as a reading mentor for two different elementary schools—both in poorer sections of the large city. She and James had fought over her doing so since he'd seen it as "unladylike." Marianne had rolled her eyes and stated, "It's volunteer work, and since you don't want me to work, I'm going to do it."

After Andrew was born, Marianne stopped volunteering until he was in pre-school. Once he was old enough, she returned to reading with the children. Last year, she was honored as Volunteer of the Year from the school district where Marianne worked. It was one of the most satisfying things to happen to her, and she immediately hung up the award plaque in the family room. She smiled, thinking of her darling granddaughter and how she'd been able to help her hone her reading skills.

"You're miles away. Everything okay?" Bella asked.

Marianne nodded. "Just lost in thought. Hey, my "bestie" girlfriends, do you want to go for a swim before breakfast?" she asked.

The three of them rose and raced to don their swimsuits, laughing like teenagers as they went.

Chapter 39

Allison lay back on the float and let her feet flop over the sides to maneuver herself around the large pool. She opened one eye to glance at where she was and smiled when she saw Marianne holding onto Bella's float at the end of the pool, laughing at something Bella said. She closed her eye and relaxed, letting her thoughts wander. Even though Marianne looked happy, Allison wondered what was worrying her. She knew herself well enough to know that she shouldn't just blurt out her question as usual but let Marianne tell them in her own time.

She thought about her sons … her handsome sons with bright blue eyes and black curly hair. Both sets were fraternal twins and her youngest by three minutes had her attention at the moment. Allison knew he was gay, and she had hinted that it was okay with her, but he hadn't come out yet. She was hoping that would happen soon, but she thought his Catholic upbringing and the manliness of Jackson were holding him back. She made up her mind to set a time up for Jackson and her to meet with him.

"Yikes! You scared me!" Allison squealed as Marianne and Bella bumped into her, nearly tipping her float over. Scrambling to steady herself, Bella caused them to screech as they too became unsteady on their floats. Soon all three were standing in the water, sputtering and laughing.

"Oh, no! My hair!" yowled Bella. Then, seeing she was tall enough to keep her hair dry, she grinned. "Thank God."

Allison stepped toward her and reached up to touch her hair. "Your hair is so pretty. Until Jackson came into my life, I didn't realize what a job it is to care for hair like yours. He says that is why he keeps his short."

"I was thinking of cutting mine short, too. But right now, it is easier just to tie it back."

"We always want someone else's hair, don't we?" Marianne said.

"I can assure you; you don't want mine," Bella laughed.

"No, I don't, but I wish I could wear my hair all the ways you wear it," admitted Allison. "I don't have your talent."

"Or hair," chuckled Marianne, holding out Allison's straight hair. The other two joined her in laughter.

The housekeeper came to the edge of the pool. "Are you ladies ready for breakfast? Shall I bring it outside since it's so pleasant and warm?"

"That would be lovely, Sarah," Marianne said.

"This is like being at a resort," crowed Allison, heading for the table. "And I'm loving it!"

Bella and Marianne smiled at Allison's enthusiasm. Because of their profession, Bella and James often had servants wait upon them. It took Bella a while to let anyone wait upon her. As a black woman, Bella was over-sensitive to the idea that others expected she should be the servant. However, James had explained to her that for many people to wait on them, particularly in third-world countries, it was a way to show respect for his and Bella's work.

Marianne eyed Allison's apparent joy at the little pleasures and thought something was to be learned from her carefree enjoyment in things that she herself took for granted. No longer being married to Jeremy opened a new way of living, and she promised to be more aware of her blessings from now on. The fear of having her cancer return made her grimace, unaware that both her friends were staring at her.

"What's going on, Marianne?" Allison asked softly. "Whatever it is, you can tell us."

"And don't tell us it is nothing, either," warned Bella.

Marianne searched her friends' eyes. "Okay. Here comes Sarah. I'll tell you after she leaves," she whispered.

Sarah served a beautiful cheese quiche with fresh fruit beside it. She placed a basket covered with a linen cloth in the center, holding warm homemade cinnamon buns. The aroma drifted over them, and pleasure filled them as they eyed the food before them.

"Spill," demanded Allison once Sarah had departed.

"There's a chance my cancer has returned. The doctor seemed pretty optimistic, but we won't know anything until he receives the biopsy report. And please, don't mention any of this to my son."

"When are you supposed to hear from the doctor?" Bella asked.

"Within the next few days…."

"Good. We'll be here to celebrate with you." At the looks from the other two, Allison said, "I'm thinking positive thoughts."

"Yes, I'm going with that, too," stated Bella.

Marianne smiled. "That's one of the reasons I love you two. You always have my back."

"Speaking about supporting each other, I can't thank you enough for attending the Me Too Movement rally with me tomorrow," Allison said, nodding to her friends. "You understand that I can't let Susan's death just be another sexual assault without railing against it in some way. It's a perfect way to express my outrage."

Bella frowned. "I can't begin to tell you what I've seen traveling with James around the world. Especially in third-world countries. The abuse against women is overwhelming."

"To be honest with you, if it hadn't been for Alyssa Milano posting 'Me Too' as a status of those sexually harassed or assaulted, and others stepping forward, I wouldn't have been aware of it." Marianne shook her head. "I was too wrapped up in what was going on in my life."

"It wouldn't have even happened without Tarana Burke's persistence in the making of the Me Too Movement in 2006." At the raised eyebrows of the other two, Allison laughed. "I looked it up."

Bella and Marianne chuckled.

"I knew I wanted to be here for this event when I realized I'd missed taking part in the Women's March on Washington to support gender equality and civil rights. It turned out to be the largest single-day demonstration in U.S. history, and I missed it," Bella lamented.

"I think it's interesting that the march took place on the first full day of Donald Trump's presidency," Marianne spoke up.

"Yes," chorused Bella and Allison.

"May I take your plates, ladies?" asked Sarah approaching the table.

"Thank you, Sarah. That would be lovely."

"May I get anyone more coffee?" Sarah asked.

"No, thank you," they said as one.

"I have no room for anything else, Sarah. Your cinnamon buns were sure delicious!" exclaimed Allison, patting her belly.

Marianne pushed back her chair. "Shall we go back to swimming and sunbathing?" asked Marianne, heading to the lounge chairs.

After she rose from her chair, Allison wrapped her arm around Bella's waist, and together they followed Marianne. When they reached her, Allison took hold of Marianne's hand. "I love you, my sister-friends."

The three of them huddled together. "We love you too, Allison," Bella said, speaking for Marianne and herself.

At that moment, a cloud passed, and the sun shone down on them like a blessing from above. They looked at each other and smiled.

Chapter 40

Allison woke the following day with a sunburn that was evident but, luckily, didn't hurt. Viewing herself in the mirror, she saw her eyes had a ring of white around them, causing a noticeable difference in her now red face. Leaning closer, Allison spotted a few freckles making their appearance. She hunted for her suntan lotion in her large cosmetic bag to apply. Her cell phone rang, interrupting her. Her heart raced as she ran to answer it.

When she saw it was Jackson, Allison eagerly picked up her phone and smiled. "Good morning, Jackson! How nice …"

Before she could say anything more, he interrupted her. "Good morning, Allison. Just hear me out, okay?

And please, don't give me an answer right now, promise?"

At the urgency in his voice, Allison's heart dropped. What was wrong? "Jackson, you're scaring me. What is it?" she pleaded.

The air between them stilled as Jackson sorted his words. "I've loved you for a long time now, Allison, and I've wanted to ask you this question ever since I realized that you had some of the same feelings for me. Will you marry me, Allison?"

Allison stood still in a state of confusion. "You want to marry me?"

"I'm hoping since you are away, you will have time and the perspective to see how wonderful things could be between us ... if we were to be married."

Yes, it was true. Allison knew that Jackson loved her. And she had fallen in love with him as well but had been too afraid to admit it. Jackson had been the constant in her life that'd kept her sane through the ups and downs of her adult years—from stepping in as a friend to her and a father to her boys after Murphy had died—and so much more. And she knew she didn't "owe" him for what he'd done, and she couldn't imagine her life without him. Yet, did that mean they needed to marry?

"Allison, are you still there?" came Jackson's voice.

"Yeah, sorry. You just took me by surprise, that's all," Allison said. "Jackson, I do love you, but marriage?"

"It's time we made our relationship official; it's the right thing to do. Don't answer me right now; just promise me you'll think about it, okay?" he pleaded.

"I will," Allison answered.

"Good. I love you, baby," Jackson said.

"I love you too," Allison responded before hearing the phone go dead. She stood in the same spot for minutes and let her mind wander into what being married to Jackson would look like. Shaking herself from her thoughts, she got out of bed to start her day with a decision to be made.

♥ ♥ ♥

Bella was surprised to feel tears drying on her face. Then, she remembered the dream she'd had earlier about James trying to tell her something. After giving his muffled message, he'd turned and walked away into the shadows. She had run after him, trying to catch up to him to find out what he'd said. But no matter how much she ran, she could never reach him. She felt alone and lost, crying for him to return to no avail.

Her sobbing was what had awakened her. She had a decision to make, and she had wanted James's guidance, which is probably why she'd dreamt about him. Bella had been waiting to speak to her friends about it. She had been looking for a sign that it was the right thing for her to do. Also, she needed to reconsider that it would be the first time leaving her daughter alone in the United States. Was this the right timing for her to go?

After the war, Viet Nam didn't magically get righted from all the damage done to the country and its people. Children had lost parents and family members who usually cared for them. Camila was only one of many who found themselves in a situation that left them scrambling for themselves. Cam had hidden behind Bella as a little girl, avoiding all the other children roaming the alley in Hanoi … lost and scouring for food.

When Bella had looked into the toddler's eyes, she felt the exchange between them and knew this child belonged to her as clearly as if she had given her birth. She vowed to do whatever it took to keep Camila by her side. And she had succeeded. Bella and James adopted her, taking her along with them on their travels. Cam had become fascinated with what they were doing, and at an early age, she studied James's every move to learn from him. Today, she was making a name for herself by expanding what her father had started.

When James died, Bella worried about Cam losing the strong connection to her father. It turned out that Bella was the one to worry about, for without James, she was utterly lost. He, along with Cam, was her everything. It had been Cam's devotion to seeing her well that had lifted her from her depression and given her the desire to return to helping children with cancer. Several years had passed since James's death, and she was looking forward to traveling again—this time to Africa with Doctors Without Borders.

She wondered what her friends would say about her idea. Thinking about them brought a sense of gratitude and love for them. It had not only been Cam who had helped her move on in life; it had been their love and support at the time as well. And, more than anything, she wanted their backing for her new venture so she could leave Cam behind with a sense of peace and purpose.

♥ ♥ ♥

Marianne felt a highness she hadn't experienced in a long time and wondered if it was because her best friends were with her. She was considering selling her large house and buying a smaller one in her son's town, 25 miles away. Marianne became excited at the thought of living closer to her granddaughter and seeing her more often.

Marianne and Isabella had a connection, and they adored each other. Anyone who saw them together commented on it. Interestingly, Isabella had turned away from Jeremy even as a baby, not wanting his attention. He, of course, had acted poorly, pushing the child's desire to be cuddled further away. Isabella had screamed at his cussing and had clung to Marianne. Rosalie had watched the entire scenario and had gone to her father-in-law, assuring him that Isabella just needed time. After all, he'd hardly paid much attention to her.

The more Marianne thought about it, decorating a new house would give her something to do and fill her days. She wanted something a little more open, with fewer boxed-off rooms than the colonial-style she had. Marianne couldn't wait for Bella and Allison to see her granddaughter in person instead of photos. Perhaps they all could drive over to see Isabella and scout out the area at the same time. Marianne became excited about the idea and threw back the bed covers.

Laughing, Marianne jumped out of bed feeling better than she had in a long time. She had a whole new life awaiting her. She pulled on her bathing suit and went down to start the coffee before Sarah arrived.

Chapter 41

Allison was the last one down for breakfast, still wearing rumpled pajamas. She hadn't slept that well, tossing and turning over whether she should marry Jackson. If Allison were younger, she probably wouldn't be struggling so much with this decision. Now that she was older, her body wasn't what it used to be, and the thought of having Jackson see her without clothes was daunting. And she hadn't had sex in so long she wondered how that would work. Her boys had kept her so busy she'd had very few dates, and Jackson was always around so that she'd let time slip by without any thought to finding a husband, replacing Murphy.

However, she knew Jackson was right. It was time for them to stop dancing around the issue, pretending that nothing was going on between them. It was time to face the fact that they loved each other. And why shouldn't they marry? It wasn't as if they had just met. In many ways, it was as if they were already married.

"Woohoo! Earth to Allison," Bella called out. "Can I pour you a cup of coffee?"

"Sorry. Yeah, that'd be great," Allison answered.

"We're out on the patio," Bella said, heading outside.

"Great. I'll be right out."

"Well, look who's up!" Marianne called out when she saw Allison.

Allison grinned sheepishly. "It's easy to sleep in knowing I'm on vacation and don't have a schedule to keep."

"Amen," agreed Bella, stretching her arms up and twisting her body in a stretch.

Marianne laughed. "It's easier when you're at someone else's house too."

"True enough," agreed Allison.

"What time do we have to be downtown for the rally? Wasn't it 11 o'clock?"

Allison nodded.

Marianne said, "That's what I thought. I've ordered a driver to take us there and back later. I told him to pick us up at 10 o'clock. We have time for a swim before breakfast at 8:30. What do you think?"

Allison and Bella nodded. "It sounds good to me," added Bella.

"You two were smart to be in your bathing suits already. I better go get mine on," Allison said.

♥ ♥ ♥

Bella was looking forward to taking part in the Me Too Movement rally. After missing out on the Women's March in Washington, she was determined to make her voice heard. Too often, it was easier to sit back and let someone else make the noises of discontent.

There was an unease in her stomach, something she'd learned meant for her to be on the alert. Bella wanted to make sure that the three of them stuck close together the entire time of being there. There was always that balance between good and evil, and this march could quickly get out of control.

Peeling off her bathing suit, Bella stood naked in front of the mirror and tried to envision how James had seen her body. He'd been insistent that her widening hips were his delight … more to love. And because he'd shown his love for Bella's body so well, any self-consciousness of the aging body changes never developed.

Turning around and viewing her backside, she scowled at her extra pounds. An understanding flashed as Bella realized that since James was no longer there to influence her thoughts, she was finding fault with her body in ways that hadn't happened before. Women were susceptible to false ideas of appearing like models, especially their bodies with little meat on them. And now, here she was, unhappy with her looks.

Bella chuckled when she remembered her grandmother's words, *"Beauty is as beauty does."* If she was going to "do," then she'd better hurry and get dressed for the march.

♥ ♥ ♥

Marianne, too, was standing in the mirror naked, lifting first one heavy breast then the other to observe the scars underneath of previous treatments for her cancer. It had never bothered Jeremy that she had them since they were pretty well hidden. She traced each scar with her finger and said a little prayer. "No more cancer, God. I want to spend time with my granddaughter. Hear?"

Marianne shook her head at her foolishness. During her early days in Boston, Marianne was determined to live a more open life than she had in Atlanta, living with her aunt. Then, learning that she had breast cancer, Marianne began using a mantra that she now repeated. "Marianne, you can do whatever is needed to heal yourself and be well." After repeating it several times, Marianne felt up to the challenge of whatever was to come.

She pulled over her head the t-shirt that Allison had made up for the march with Susan's photo, name, and date of death across the front. Patting it down her front, Marianne studied Susan's picture in the mirror. Susan certainly had been a knockout. Although she had been careless about other people's feelings, often dismissing them, Susan didn't deserve to be murdered. No woman or anybody deserved to be sexually abused or abused in any way. The thought of her granddaughter being treated similarly made Marianne even more eager to participate in the rally and show her support against it.

She headed down the stairs to wait for the limo driver.

Chapter 42

Allison smiled as she went down the stairs and saw Marianne and Bella standing there in their bright, chartreuse green t-shirts. The three of them were going to look like limes with feet, Allison thought and laughed out loud.

Marianne and Bella looked her way and smiled. "What's so funny?" asked Bella.

"I'm looking at the three of us in our t-shirts. It's going to be hard not to notice us, that's for sure," Allison answered.

"Well, if that's the case, let's make the best of it," chimed in Marianne, "and make this rally count for Susan."

Unexpectantly, tears formed. When the limo driver pulled up front, the three swiped at their eyes before heading to the limo. Bella was glad to see that it was the same driver who'd met her at the airport. "Hi, William, it's nice to see you."

"And you, too, Miz Bella," he said. Turning to Marianne, he asked, "Are you ready to go, Miz Marianne?"

Marianne nodded and reached for her thermal bag, holding chilled water bottles. The three of them loaded into the back of the limo, light-hearted and eager for the march.

"William, the rally is starting and ending at City Hall. Where do you think the best place is to drop us off?" asked Marianne.

"There's a smoke shop a block away, not far from City Hall. I can pull in there and let you off. That will be a good place to pick you up as well."

"That'll be fine, William," agreed Marianne smiling.

Allison was intrigued by the interaction between Marianne and William. Although they spoke formally to each other, there was an intimacy and respect for each other. They were friends! Allison realized.

The times that Allison had been to Atlanta before, it always had been for a significant event with minimal downtime to relax—Marianne's wedding, Andrew's baptism, Jeremy's father and then his mother's funerals, and several large fundraisers for Jeremy's unsuccessful push into politics. The three spent a few holidays together but not often because Bella was usually traveling, and Allison's boys and Murphy's family always had something going on that required her attention.

Already, by spending a few days here with Marianne and Bella, Allison was getting a sense of the slower pace that the South held. Surrounded by Marianne's luxurious way of living with black servants serving them, Allison felt at odds with the idea that servants didn't mind waiting on them. The divide between white and black was still evident after all this time, and she thought about her relationship with Jackson. Allison loved Jackson, and her boys thought of him as their father. She wondered if the South of today would have allowed that when their relationship had begun. Southie could be challenging for anyone black, but she'd bet that being black in the South with a white woman thirty years ago would have been harsher.

Allison's thoughts turned to Susan. God, she still missed her! She smiled at the remembered boldness of how Susan treated others by her overblown sense of entitlement. Men had seemed to like the challenge she presented until they didn't. Susan could never understand that her actions toward others weren't always okay with them and could entice anger. Yet, Susan didn't deserve to die, no matter how much she angered anyone.

♥ ♥ ♥

Bella shifted in her seat. The feeling she'd had earlier returned, setting off an alarm. "Let's make sure we stick together, and no one gets lost. You know how easily that can happen in a big crowd."

"That's why I picked this color for our shirts. I figured we could easily pick each other out of a crowd with it," Allison said.

"Do you know who is going to be speaking before the rally begins?" Bella asked.

Allison and Marianne eyed each other and shook their heads. "We'll find out when we get there," Marianne responded.

The closer they drove to City Hall, the more women they saw wearing tee-shirts stamped with "Me Too" milling around. Many were hugging each other and laughing like longtime friends, filled with pride in their camaraderie.

William pulled in behind the smoke shop and let them out. Marianne handed each of them a carrier holding a bottle of cold water they could wear around their neck. "Thanks, William. I'll let you know when to pick us up."

"Very good, Miz Marianne." He waited outside the vehicle until he could no longer see them.

Bella fell behind the others, filled with anxiety. She turned back in time to see the limo's back end turn the corner. There was no turning back now. She sighed as she hurried to catch up with Allison and Marianne. Bella realized then that it would be up to her to keep them in sight, for they seemed unaware that she wasn't with them.

♥ ♥ ♥

Marianne was proud that she was a part of this exciting group protesting the inequality of women and the abuse they suffered at the hands of men. She thought about how it must seem to Bella. By being black, she had even more grievances. Marianne looked back to see Bella rushing toward them and wondered what had caught her attention to delay her. Allison stopped, and together they waited for Bella to catch up.

Marianne held out her hand to Bella, and when she got close enough, Marianne grabbed her and pulled her close so the three of them could hug. "We're the three amigos now and forever!" cried Allison.

Caught up in Allison's enthusiasm, Marianne pulled them closer. Several women approached them from behind and introduced themselves. Soon, more women joined in, and before they knew it, they were surrounded by women of all ages and colors. While chatting, they moved to the stage in front of City Hall as a group.

A low, musical voice sailed out from a microphone in the middle of the stage, where a tall black woman welcomed them all. Marianne had no idea who she was. But the speaker was well enough known to have drawn news reporters and photographers, some of whom skirted the crowd while a few made their way through the women asking questions.

The woman on stage asked a few women in the crowd to tell her why they were there. Suddenly, the woman on stage was pointing at the three of them.

"You there, in the bright shirts, tell us why you're here, please."

Allison raised her voice. "My roommate was murdered."

"I see that you have put her face on your shirts. I want the others to see that this gives even greater attention to your roommate's abuse. Will you three please come up on the stage? Remember, the more that we can speak for the dead, the louder our voices will be heard."

Chapter 43

Allison looked to the others. "Ready to do this?"

Bella and Marianne didn't look too happy but nodded their assent. The three mounted the stairs of the stage and found themselves wrapped in the arms of the large woman leading the rally.

"Thank you so much for agreeing to share your story, ladies. So tell us what happened to your roommate."

After Allison told her story, there was a hush as people began to realize the killer had never been found and brought to justice. Flashbulbs popped as they stood lined up on the stage, facing the audience so all could glimpse Susan's picture on their shirts.

Suddenly, a male voice called out, "Aren't you the 'three bitches'?"

An angry female voice shouted, "Who are you calling a bitch?"

He answered, "No, not me. It was a nickname given to the three of them. Ask them; they'll tell you."

Resigned to the fact that they were in the limelight despite not wanting to be, Allison, Bella, and Marianne groaned and nodded.

When Allison finished, the crowd went wild, demanding that the one who had called them that name be found and prosecuted, demonstrating their sisterhood, and giving the gathering a focus.

The leader called them to order. "Ladies, we're here today to give voice *respectfully* to our demand to be treated fairly as women of value no matter our age or color. Our Me Too Movement demands justice for those who have or would abuse us. We are no longer going to sit back and be quiet. We are no longer going to give our power away. We are here to empower sexually assaulted individuals through empathy and solidarity through strength in number (especially young and vulnerable women), by visibly demonstrating how many have survived sexual assault and harassment, especially in the workplace."

The crowd roared and began clapping their hands in rhythm, "No More. Enough is enough."

Allison, Bella, and Marianne made their way off the stage and were greeted by smiling women patting their backs in encouragement. Some said thank you for speaking up for Susan. They pushed forward, and upon finally reaching the edge of the crowd, they looked at each other in dismay. Flashbulbs popped, and several reporters rushed forward.

Allison and Bella held them off with "No Comment" while Marianne busily punched in William's cell phone number.

Settling themselves in the back of the limo, they breathed a sigh of relief. "I never expected that to happen!" exclaimed Allison.

Bella and Marianne eyed her, saying nothing, resigned to what had taken place. Then, Bella said, "We're never going to live that name down, are we?"

Marianne covered her mouth and began to giggle. "I can just imagine the teasing that Jeremy is going to get at the club."

"He's not the only one who is going to be teased over this," stated Bella, remembering what'd happened years ago at the hospital where she'd worked.

"I know Jackson is not going to be happy to have Susan's death still unresolved aired in the public media. It makes his entire department look bad," worried Allison.

"Who knows, maybe his department and all the others around the country will open the door to using new technology to bag the killers of cold cases and bring them to justice," said Marianne.

"That's you, Marianne, always looking on the bright side of things," Bella said.

"How do you think I survived living with all of Jeremy's misdeeds?" Marianne responded. "You have to believe something good will come out of all of this."

"You're right, Marianne," agreed Allison. "We wanted Susan's death to count for something. Maybe, this is how. And if being called the 'three bitches' gets us the attention we need to solve her case, then so be it."

Bella studied Allison and Marianne. Then she lifted her water bottle and tapped it against theirs. "Right on. Here's to the 'three bitches.'"

They listened to William chuckling from the front of the limo and joined in. Then, they leaned in for a group hug. Instead of being upset, each felt a thrill that their actions might bring to the forefront a greater demand to find and punish those who have abused or killed their victims.

♥ ♥ ♥

Allison's cell phone began to chirp, and she pulled it from her pocket to see that it was Jackson. She looked at Bella and Marianne. "It's Jackson. He might have seen us on television. Should I answer it?"

"Better now than never. See what he wants," suggested Marianne.

"Hi, Jackson. What's up?"

"I see you girls are making a name for yourselves once again. By stirring things up, you need to be careful. All it takes is one lunatic to do something stupid."

"I know. We'll be careful."

"And, baby, a word of warning. Bringing attention to Susan's unsolved death hasn't earned you any points with the boys in the department. But I think the Captain is making it a priority to review the case again."

"Oh, Jackson! That's wonderful!"

"Bye, baby, I've got to run."

♥ ♥ ♥

Bella's phone rang next, and she picked it up with a smile. Camilla.

"Hi, darling, how are you?" Bella asked.

"Wow, Mom, I just saw you and Aunt Allison and Aunt Marianne on television! You're making headlines on all the news, and I wanted to tell you that I'm very proud of you all. I think good things will come from your story. Good going, Mom!"

"Thank you, darling."

"Have to run, Mom. I'll catch up with you later. Love you."

♥ ♥ ♥

Marianne picked up her ringing cell phone to hear, "Now you've done it! Made a complete fool of me at the club with you and friends wearing those silly tee-shirts with that woman's face on it. She was nothing but a slut, Marianne!"

"Jeremy, how can you say that? You never even met Susan."

"Don't be silly. I heard about her, and that's enough for me to know what she was."

"Is that why you are calling me ... to tell me that?"

"No, we need to meet with the lawyer again. There's some question about some stock you own and didn't report. Are you trying to cheat me, Marianne?"

"You know better than that, Jeremy. I'll set the meeting up after Allison and Bella leave."

"But ...!

"I can't hear you ... we're going into a blind spot," she ended, winking at her friends. "As you can see, ladies, money isn't everything," stated Marianne with a shake of her head.

Chapter 44

Allison crept out of bed and raced to the window to see what was causing all the racket outside. Two television trucks were parked in the driveway, and several people with microphones in their hands were standing around while photographers set their equipment in place. A man was directing a younger version of himself to move his camera closer to the front door so that he could get a closeup of whoever answered the door.

Allison knelt to hide from her bird's eye view but stayed close to the window to hear everything going on. A loud knock on the front door reverberated throughout the house. Allison heard tiny steps below her bedroom scurry across the marble hallway and stop by the front door. Soon, the door opened, and she heard Sarah say in a formidable scolding tone, "Go on, leave us alone. You're not welcome here."

The man mumbled something, and Sarah challenged, "Where are your manners, boy? Go on now … Git!"

After Sarah slammed the door shut with a thud, Allison raised her eyebrows in surprise and chuckled. Sarah was no one you wanted to fool with … she was a tough cookie when she had to be.

Allison rose from her spot and hurried downstairs. Again, she was the last one down. Marianne and Bella were already there, huddled at the kitchen table, talking.

"Hey, sleepyhead, did the press wake you?" Marianne asked.

"Enough to hear Sarah tell them to git," laughed Allison

Bella chuckled. "Sarah is a good one to have on your side. That woman can be downright scary. She wore the same look my grandmother did when I misbehaved, and that, you don't fool with!"

Marianne smiled. "I don't know what I'd do without her, that's for sure. Listen, I received a call from one of our local television stations to interview us. I told her I'd have to talk to you before I could give her an answer. What do you think?"

"To talk about Susan?" asked Allison.

"I'm assuming so," replied Marianne.

"What's the point?" asked Bella. "What could we add that hasn't already been said? And I'm tired of being referred to as the bitches."

"I agree," Marianne said. "I hate the name-calling, too. But we need to decide together what we're going to do. Allison? What do you think?"

"You're in this because of me, and I'm sorry about the name-calling, but I think we should say something about it … how important it is not to put a person in a box by labeling her, as Jeremy just did with Susan." At the disappointed looks on Bella's and Marianne's faces, Allison added, "But maybe we can do it through a joint letter we write together. What do you say?"

"Hmm, I like that idea," Marianne said. "What do you think, Bella?"

"Count me in. I'll do anything not to be in the limelight again. Besides, I think Allison has a point about the damage labeling people can do. God knows how that goes. Try being black," Bella said, shaking her head.

"Try being anything these days," grumbled Allison, aware of what her son could suffer if he came out as a gay man.

"So we're going to do this?" Marianne asked.

"Okay then, call the reporter back, Marianne, and tell her she can expect our letter by the end of the day. Does that work for you two?" Allison asked.

"Sounds good," Bella said.

"Yup, me too," Marianne said as she rose to call the reporter.

Luckily Marianne's backyard was private, enclosed by tall cement walls similar to others in warm climates. Sarah brought breakfast outside to the terrace, and they sipped their coffee and ate as Marianne jotted down notes of what they would write for the reporter.

"Let's keep it simple," Bella teased, eying Allison enough to make her laugh.

"I know; I know I can get off track," Allison admitted good-naturedly.

"How about this, then," suggested Marianne. "We start by stating why we're here—to honor Susan and to bring her death to the foreground as the abuse it was and something we women are no longer willing to put up with without a fight."

"What about men? When we looked up the statistics on abuse, we know that men are also sexually abused, too," stated Allison.

Bella responded, "Let's just stick with Susan's story. We're here to honor her, as Marianne said, and bring attention to what the Me Too Movement stands for. Let's be honest. We know that the reporter wants to speak with us because we were called the 'three bitches', and she's trying to get us riled up to make this a juicy story for her bloodthirsty readers to pass around. Something more to be angry about if you know what I mean."

"I don't want that!" exclaimed Allison. "I can see it now … 'Was Susan really a slut?' I'm not going to expose Susan in that light."

"Okay, I have to agree with you both. Let's put our heads together again and come up with what we want to say," Marianne said.

It took nearly two hours to hone down the letter for the reporter. Marianne stood and read back what they had created:

Dear Ms. Williamson,

Thank you for the opportunity to acknowledge Susan for the beautiful soul she was. She didn't deserve to be assaulted and murdered. We protest against the outrageous statistics that one in five women in the United States suffers completed or attempted rape, and globally, nearly one in three women are subjected to abuse in some form.

We are honored to participate in the Me Too Movement that protests sexual assault and harassment. By raising our voices, we hope to demonstrate the empowerment reached when we demand loving treatment of ourselves and others, not accepting anything less. We believe that by women combining our voices, there is a greater chance of teaching our young girls and boys that they have a right to grow up in a safe environment without the worry of being sexually abused or labeled in a negative way.

Sincerely,
Allison Murphy, Bella Kowasaki, Marianne Loveland

Chapter 45

Allison sat alone at the poolside table, lost in thoughts about Jackson wanting them to be married. She was unaware that Marianne and Bella were calling out to her. Climbing out of the pool, they approached Allison, dripping wet.

"Hey, Allison, what's going on? You're very quiet," Bella said.

Allison's face warmed. "Oh, not much…."

"C'mon, we don't believe that. Your head has been in the clouds for a few days now. What is it, Allison?" Marianne pressed.

Allison was embarrassed, and her cheeks reddened. Then, her words spilled out, "Jackson wants us to get married. He's waiting for my decision, and I haven't decided yet."

"My God, girl! What is there to decide? It's not like it would be that much of a stretch since you're like an old married couple already!" exclaimed Bella. "Besides, that gorgeous man has been in love with you forever. I think it'd be fantastic if you two married."

"Me, too!" Marianne agreed as she neared Allison and sat next to her. "So, what's the issue?" she asked, leaning in and wrapping her arm around Allison's shoulders.

Allison's eyes watered. "I love Jackson; you know that I do. Do you remember when I inherited all that money from Susan? Back then, I spent weeks with her lawyer and my new accountant learning about the stock market and other investments and setting up a trust fund. After Murphy died, both my lawyer and accountant said that if I were ever to remarry, they would help protect my investments."

"Are you worried about Jackson taking money from you?" questioned Bella in astonishment, plopping into the empty seat beside Allison.

"Absolutely not! Quite the opposite. Jackson thinks I live off the investments I've made from Murphy's pretty hefty life insurance. I've lived simply in the large house that the mortgage insurance paid for after Murphy's death. I've been very careful not to touch much of the money I'd inherited from Susan, so Jackson has no idea I am more than financially sound. And you know Jackson well enough by now to know his pride won't allow him to be indebted to me or willing to accept large financial gifts. I promised myself that once the boys were through their schooling and on their own, I would kick up my heels and travel some. How do you think that is going to work with Jackson?"

"Sweetie, I've seen how you have struggled not to overdo and spoil your boys. And I commend you for that. When my aunt left me her money, she left some advice for me. Part of the agreement to accept her wealth was to keep one account in my name only, a trust fund that no one could touch. It also allowed me to spend my money without my husband's approval. And from what you've said, I believe that is what your people did for you."

Allison nodded. "And because I'm not married, I didn't have to answer to anyone how I spent my money. And I like that freedom. So what's going to happen if I marry Jackson?"

Bella spoke up. "You tell that handsome man your plans to travel and that you have invested and saved money so that you can do it together. And ask him if he has a problem with that."

"Yes, I believe being honest and upfront is the answer, too. Jackson doesn't need to know the total amount of your investments at this point. File your taxes, separately too. I have a feeling Jackson is not going to let what you have to say hold him back from wanting to make you his wife."

"I hope you're right," lamented Allison. Then, she chuckled. "This is the most inane conversation—to be worried that my wealth will destroy my chance to live happily with a man I've loved for years."

♥ ♥ ♥

Bella smiled at Allison's statement. She wondered if she would have the strength to start over again with a new man in her life. Allison was lucky in that respect since she and Jackson had been in each other's lives for more than 20 years, so it wouldn't be like starting their relationship from scratch.

Bella missed James and the security he gave her just by being in her life. There was something to be said for a solid, loving, respectful union completing one's life. However, Bella thought that no one could ever measure up to James, and she'd already made a conscious decision to fill his void by working with children again.

"Do you still miss James?" Allison asked.

"Every day," Bella answered. "There are days that I wonder how I'm going to get through them without him by my side."

"I know what you mean, except what I'd do without all my boys and their friends always around. I like all the noise and roughhousing."

"Have you thought about going back to work, Bella?" Marianne asked. "I know how much you love children."

"And how much they love you!" added Allison.

Bella ducked her head, then looked at them, smiling. "I was planning on telling you my news later, but now is as good a time as ever…."

"What is it?" Allison and Marianne chorused.

"I've tentatively signed up for Doctors Without Borders. It will be the first time I'll be in another country since James' death, leaving Cam alone here in the United States. I haven't told her yet that I'm going. I wanted to see what you thought about it first since I'm hoping I can rely on you both if she needs something and can't reach me. Will you do that?"

"Of course," they agreed in unison.

"So when would you be leaving, and where are you going to be?" Marianne asked.

Bella's face brightened, and her eyes shone. I won't leave until after the Christmas holidays, so Cam and I will have enough time to get used to my going. I'll be in Mozambique."

"I've certainly heard of Doctors Without Borders and know they work on ships, but I don't know much more," Allison confessed.

"Doctors Without Borders began in May 1968 when a group of young doctors decided to help victims of wars and major disasters. That humanitarianism reinvented the concept of emergency aid. It was then that, for the first time, television broadcasted scenes of children dying from hunger in remote corners of the world. Those pictures had always touched James' heart, and he'd wanted to join them, but then we adopted Cam. After a while on the road with her, he wanted to raise Cam in the United States."

"Do you have trepidations about going?" Marianne asked.

"Only about leaving Cam behind."

"Well, we can help you out there. The boys adore Cam, and she is always welcomed at our house," Allison said.

"As she is here," added Marianne.

"You two are my best friends, and I'm so grateful that we met all those years ago," Bella said, tears in her eyes.

♥ ♥ ♥

"And here we are today still in a waiting room … the waiting room of life where we look at how we want to spend the rest of our lives before we die," said Marianne in a soft voice. "Each of us is at a crossroads in life. Allison, you have decided to marry and share your later years with someone you love, and Bella, you have chosen to live your passion for nursing sick children. I have ended an unhealthy relationship by divorcing Jeremy despite loving him."

"Do you realize how courageous that makes us?" Bella said.

Smiling, Allison confessed, "It going to take courage to have Jackson see me naked."

Marianne and Bella laughed.

"Yes, there is that too," agreed Bella. "We're at the stage where everything is sliding downward."

"And outward," added Allison, patting her tummy.

A cloud passed Marianne's brow and then was gone. "I've thought of my aunt recently, and I have to give her credit. She said a few things, which I didn't appreciate at the time—like making sure I had financial freedom."

"What else?" Bella asked.

Marianne frowned. "She said that not everyone who was nice to me was my friend, and that was just part of life. Since my divorce, that thought has come up several times when I've walked into the club, and a group of women and sometimes men stop talking as soon as they see me. I've even overheard some women say nasty things about me in the ladies' locker room."

"Ouch, that hurts. I'm so sorry, Marianne," Allison said.

Bella patted Marianne's hand. "Me too. Just remember you have us."

Marianne smiled. "Yes, and I'm grateful for that."

Allison's brows pushed together in thought. "My mother told me to spend as much time with my kids as I could when they were little because they would soon be gone," Allison said. "And she said not to worry if the house didn't get straightened. It was more important to give them my time."

"Your house always looks nice and clean when I've seen it," Bella said.

Allison sighed. "Clean, but not always neat. Early on, I realized that's impossible to do with four boys born within two and a half years. All little boys like to do is wrestle! And big boys too!"

Bella and Marianne laughed. They knew Allison's tribe was always ribbing each other, fooling around.

"What about you, Bella? Any words of wisdom?" Marianne asked.

Bella chuckled. "My grandmother was a lot like your Sarah. She was no one's fool and demanded respect. She was always telling me, 'Don't you sass me, or you'll wish you hadn't!' And those were fighting words."

Marianne and Allison chuckled.

Bella continued. "She'd say, 'No black woman should accept color as an excuse not to be where she wants to be in life.' She's the one who encouraged me to go to college and get my doctorate."

"Wow, what a savvy lady. What did she do for a living?" asked Allison.

"Worked as a maid for a wealthy family, and that is where she learned how to invest her money. Sometimes, she'd even take in other people's laundry for extra money," stated Bella with pride.

"What a great inspiration she must have been," acknowledged Marianne.

Bella smiled. "Yes, she was and still is."

The three sat in thought, glad for the advice they'd received years back.

Chapter 46

Allison woke to the hush of daybreak and relaxed back amid the pillows, unwilling to get out of bed just yet. She thought of Marianne's reference to the waiting room the three of them were in now and wondered what would happen if Marianne's results showed that her cancer was back. Allison would never want Marianne to be alone going through this. She knew how much her mother-in-law appreciated Allison being there with her at the end of her fight with cancer. And, if necessary, she'd do the same for Marianne.

Mozambique was so far away and a dangerous place to be. Wonder if anything happened to Bella? Allison closed her eyes and began to pray. Despite being catholic, she didn't believe that trouble or sickness was a punishment like some believed. Allison's own faith was that God wanted all humankind to be happy and healthy, and it was humans who got in the way of that.

Suddenly anxious to hear Jackson's voice, Allison picked up her phone and punched his number in. When it rang and rang, and he didn't answer, she felt alone and lost as if she were a small island in an endless sea. She knew that her worries without faith put her there without him near. Drawing in a deep breath, she closed her eyes and sat still, meditating.

♥ ♥ ♥

Bella awoke with a sense of contentment she hadn't felt in a long time. She was so thankful that Allison and Marianne would be there for Cam while she was away. She trusted them both, and should anything happen to her, Bella knew they would help Cam set things right.

Thinking of being so far away made Bella's heart thump in anticipation, but she knew without a doubt that she needed to return to nursing children or she would go mad. Being with them gave her stability both mentally and physically. And she hoped that Cam might join her for a few weeks of her vacation time. Just the thought of them being together in that manner lifted her spirits even higher.

Having worked with sick people of all ages, she was aware of all the discomforts that aging brought on, and with her family history of arthritis and heart issues, she wanted to get the most out of life while she could.

Bella's thoughts turned to Marianne. She had seen Marianne wince in pain when she'd bumped her body against the edge of the pool, and it didn't bode well. Maybe something else caused it, and she prayed that was so. If Marianne's results weren't good and her health took a turn for the worst, Bella would arrange to be with her at the end. That was never a question in her mind.

♥ ♥ ♥

Marianne woke with a disquieting sense that something was wrong. Fear made her raise her hand and caress first one breast and then the other. Her relief was tangible—all clear. No lumps. Then, she felt a twitch and moved her hand underneath her arm. Her eyes filled as she felt a lump in her lymph gland.

Goddammit, no! she cried silently.

Anger filled Marianne as she thought of her beautiful granddaughter. She would do everything she could to overcome her cancer to spend time with her. But innately, she realized there was just so much she could do.

Marianne's mind traveled to her friends. Thank God Allison and Bella were here. She'd need their help to get through the first few days of her diagnosis to get things in place. Several years ago, she'd gotten their permission to be co-executors of her will, and they'd agreed, amidst not wanting to think of what it meant.

Marianne wiped her tears away, and reaching across the bed and coming up empty-handed, she thought how foolish it had been of her not to have gotten another dog for herself as she'd wanted. Dogs were such a comfort. Her last dog had died a year ago, and Marianne missed having one around. However, if she lived long enough, she'd get another poodle as all her dogs had been. With that thought in mind, she felt better and went down to start the coffee.

♥ ♥ ♥

Allison and Bella chuckled over the text message that Marianne had received, showing her granddaughter with a messy face making cookies with her mother.

"How adorable!" Allison exclaimed.

"Such a beauty," announced Bella.

Marianne beamed. "I love her so much."

It was then that the phone call came from Marianne's doctor.

At the expression on Marianne's face, Bella asked, "Do you want us to leave?"

Shaking her head no, Marianne answered. "Hello, Dr. Edmonton." Silence. "Yes, I can see you this afternoon. What time?" Silence. "Yes, I'll see you at 2 o'clock."

Tears filled Marianne's eyes. "The news isn't good. Will you come with me to the doctor's office?"

Allison and Bella clustered around Marianne. "Of course."

"If it turns out that we have cancer, we'll fight it together," Allison said.

Marianne chuckled despite herself. "We?"

"Absolutely," agreed Bella. "All for one, one for all."

"I asked you to come with me because the doctor wants to talk to me about an experimental drug. I'd like to see what you both think about it, too."

"There are some very effective ones they've come up with recently. I'd be happy to give you my opinion," Bella said.

"And I'm always willing to give my opinion on anything," Allison said, making the other two smile.

Sarah approached. "Are you ladies ready for your coffee on the terrace?"

Chapter 47

Two o'clock came before they were emotionally ready for what lay ahead. Marianne drove because she knew the way to the medical center, and she sat tense behind the wheel. Allison and Bella made small talk, keeping the conversation away from the idea that Marianne's cancer had returned. It was a hot, muggy day, and by the time they walked from the parking garage into the doctor's office, they were relieved to be in the air conditioning.

Allison noticed the receptionist behind the glass partition wore the same set expression that she'd seen too many times on the faces of those who had treated her mother-in-law … seemingly braced for the worst. As she had before, she wondered if that expression changed once they left the office.

Allison marveled at Marianne's determined demeanor to treat this visit as nothing more than a simple check-up. Yet, studying her more closely, Allison saw the fear in her eyes. Catching Marianne's attention, Allison smiled and winked at her, sending encouragement. Marianne smiled back.

♥ ♥ ♥

Bella grabbed one of the pamphlets from the bin by the registration desk. She wanted to see if she could find any new information about treating cancer. Bella had worked with cancer patients most of her life and knew that anything could change as cures progressed. As she had seen many times ... miracles happen every day.

Most of what she read, she had already known. Bella was curious to see what Dr. Edmonton would propose. Because of Marianne's history of cancer, Bella hoped that Marianne would be open to trying the experimental drug. She didn't think Marianne had anything to lose, but she would see what the doctor had to say.

Bella followed Marianne and Allison into the doctor's office and waited there with them for the doctor to arrive. They heard his rushing footsteps before they saw him. He opened the door with a flourish, and his energy and enthusiasm for life surrounded him like a comfortable bathrobe. His light blue eyes twinkled, and his rounded body filled the doorway. Bella immediately liked him and sensed he was someone who cared about each of his patients.

"Marianne!" he yelled with joy. "I see you brought a posse with you! Good. Very good."

"These are my dear friends. I've told you about them, Dr. Edmonton."

"Yes, indeed," he said. He clapped Marianne on the shoulder affectionately and shook Bella and Allison's hand as they introduced themselves. "Aw right, ladies. Let's get to it."

Dr. Edmonton walked to the back of the room and mounted the x-ray so that all could see. "You can see the lump you have in your lymph gland and a few smaller ones spread around your body. I'm not so worried about those, but I am with the one under your arm. However, I think that we can get rid of that with radiation. A new drug has been proven to clear up some smaller cancer cells, which is organically based. You might know something about how that works, Bella?"

Bella said, "Yes, my husband believed in using natural remedies as much as possible."

Dr. Edmonton nodded. "I'm excited about the results I've seen with this new drug, and I'd like to use it on you, Marianne." He said assuredly, "I think it can do the trick."

"So what does this involve?" asked Allison. "Does she need to be hospitalized for it?"

"No, Marianne will come in as an outpatient for the radiation treatment as well as injections of the new drug. We should know within the first two weeks whether this is going to work."

Relief spread through the three of them. Seeing this, Dr. Edmonton added, "It will help her heal faster with you two ladies here with her."

Shaking her head, Marianne said, "I can't ask you to do that, Bella and Allison."

Allison held up her hand, "If things were reversed and it was me in your situation, would you help me through it?"

Marianne nodded.

"When is Marianne's first appointment, Dr. Edmonton? We're in this together," Bella announced.

"I have things ready now if you're set to go, Marianne."

With those words said, it was the beginning of Marianne's healing sessions, bringing in a greater closeness between the three of them.

Chapter 48

The three of them were dragging as they left the medical center. Marianne had had her cancer treatment, and it was clear that she needed to rest. She was leaning into Bella as she held her purse open, searching for the car keys to hand to Allison so that she could drive them home.

As Allison stood waiting for the keys, she saw out of the corner of her eye a dark figure rushing toward them. Before she could react, she was shoved hard into the other two. Allison struggled to stay standing and failing to do so, the three of them toppled over each other and hit the pavement in a pile.

Allison was the first to pull herself free. Sputtering, she yelled, "What the hell? What did you do that for?"

Turning to face her attacker, Allison was shocked to see an unkempt man in a hoodie standing several feet away, grinning at her. He was drunk and wore a crazed look on his face. A flash of recognition came to her, and slowly she came to see it was Matt, Susan's boyfriend from years ago.

"Matt, is that you? Why are you here?" she asked, confused.

When he stepped forward, he lifted a gun that had been hidden and aimed it at Allison.

"Matt, stop! What are you doing?" pleaded Allison.

"You couldn't let things be, could you? You had to come to Atlanta and whine about no one finding Susan's killer. Well, look closely because here he is! It was me who killed Susan that night."

"But why? I thought you loved her?"

He laughed. "That night, I tried to tell her how much I loved her, and do you know what she did? She laughed at me. The bitch told me that I couldn't be in love with her because I had refused to take her to bed."

"Oh no, Matt, please tell me it wasn't you who killed Susan."

"She treated me like shit. The slut deserved to die."

Allison heard Marianne and Bella behind her, scrambling to get upright. She was afraid their movement might threaten Matt, and she tried to think of how she could draw his attention away from them. But her mind was a blank.

"Stop, right where you are, bitches! Don't make a move, or I'll shoot," he demanded.

Not believing what she was seeing, Allison saw Jackson approaching, inching his way forward with another cop beside him.

"Jackson, what are you doing here?" yelled Allison, hoping to draw Matt's attention away from her best friends.

When Matt turned to look, Allison made her move and rushed forward, knocking him over. A shot rang out, and everyone stilled for a moment, each checking to see which one of them had been shot. Then they heard Matt crying out, holding his leg high. "I've been shot!"

When Allison saw he'd shot himself in the foot, she bit back a smile and moved away from him at the same time she saw Jackson pick up Matt's gun and tuck it into his pants.

Jackson turned to his partner. "Call the ambulance and tell the police we have him in custody," urged Jackson. Business over, he turned to Allison and opened his arms wide.

Allison ran into Jackson's waiting arms. "How did you know where to find us?"

"Don't you ever check your phone?" he asked as he leaned down and traced his finger alongside her cheek. "I left you messages, and when you didn't answer, I went crazy thinking you might be in trouble. It looks like I was right."

"I don't understand...."

"Your cell phone lets me know your location, Allison."

"Ooh."

Sirens were heard coming closer. In a matter of minutes, the local police and a couple of reporters arrived. Jackson pulled Allison closer. "Take Marianne home. It looks like she's had enough for today. I'll meet you back at her house as soon as possible, and I'll fill you ladies in on all that's happened in the past few days. I'll arrange for the police to interview you tomorrow. You all are safe now."

Allison looked deep into Jackson's eyes and saw his concern and love for her and love for Bella and Marianne, too, as he acknowledged them. She knew how lucky she was to have him in her life.

♥ ♥ ♥

It was fortunate that Bella was strong enough to protect Marianne from the worst of the fall. However, for the added effort she'd made, she'd be stiff and sore for the next few days. She only hoped all this upset and excitement wouldn't affect Marianne much more than usual after her treatment.

She couldn't believe Jackson was here and had rescued them from Matt. Bella remembered that Allison had talked about Matt being one of Susan's dates shortly after Susan's death. Allison had been convinced at the time that he had nothing to do with her murder. If it were true that Matt was the killer, how had the police missed it?

As soon as Allison pulled the car into Marianne's house, they wearily climbed out and headed inside.

Bella covered Marianne with a soft cashmere throw as she lay on the couch in the family room. Marianne had insisted on being there instead of her bedroom, not wanting to miss out on Jackson explaining how things had come about. Bella didn't blame her for that.

Meanwhile, Bella kept a careful eye on Allison to watch for any delayed shock reaction. Allison had been the one threatened by Matt, and Bella knew Allison was mulling over the realization that Matt had been Susan's killer.

Bella understood how treating someone poorly in any fashion had the possibility of adverse reactions. Susan had paid a heavy price for her acts of unkindness, and the entire situation made Bella sad.

As she had aged, Bella's sensitivity to what was happening in the world made her sad nearly every day. It seemed as if all civility had fallen by the wayside, especially with those in power leading the way. It was hard to believe that adults were acting like misbehaving children with their name-calling and blaming others for things not going their way.

Bella was glad to be going back to the children who needed her help in healing. With that thought, Bella received the message from James that she had been seeking. She saw him clearly in her mind smiling and nodding his head.

♥ ♥ ♥

As soon as her head hit the pillow, Marianne felt herself drifting off. She felt more at peace than she had in years with her friends close by. And where had Jackson come from? He was a good man. She was glad that Allison would marry him because it was evident how much Jackson loved her. And it had not gone unnoticed the caring she'd seen for her and Bella when he'd looked their way.

Before slipping away completely into her dreams, she had a sense that she'd be able to survive a bit longer, giving her more time with her granddaughter. She smiled at that thought. She had so much to share with her and teach her … things only a grandmother could get away with.

♥ ♥ ♥

Jackson mounted the marble steps and knocked at the door. Sarah greeted him with a smile. "They're waiting for you in the family room. Follow me." Once at the doorway of the comfy room, Sarah asked, "May I bring you a glass of freshly made lemonade?"

Jackson walked into the room, looking tired though happy to see them. After kissing Allison thoroughly on the lips, he plopped himself down in the comfy chair waiting for him. Sarah handed him his drink, and then he began…

"After you ladies were on television at the Me Too Movement event, the captain became obsessed with finding Susan's killer. We put out several announcements and a reward for anyone who could give us further information. Naturally, it took us time to sort out the wrong information, and then came two different people who said they'd seen a man arguing with Susan in the alleyway that night. Each described their person, and they matched. We had, of course, pulled out Susan's cold file and begun to go through it when we came upon a note that Murphy had circled with question marks. It was about Matt, who had no alibi but had an unusual number of good references."

The three of them became captivated by Jackson's story. "Why did Murphy circle that?" asked Allison.

Jackson chuckled. "It was too good to be true, which turned out to be the case. Usually, we find at least one negative thing about a person, but not Matt? That meant we should keep an eye on him."

"So, how did you know where to find him?" Bella asked.

"It was easy to do. We did the same as we had with you, Allison—his cell phone."

"Right," nodded Bella in understanding.

"As you know, Matt turned into an unreliable drunk, and we couldn't get him to cooperate. So we needed to follow him to see if he would slip up. When I saw that he had gotten a flight to Atlanta, I began to put two and two together, and that's when I tried to reach Allison."

"And you couldn't reach her because she was with me in the hospital where we can't use our cell phones," added Marianne.

Jackson nodded.

"Oh my! I'm so grateful that you got here in time to save us from that crazy man, Jackson, " Marianne added.

"Yes," echoed the other two. "Thank God!"

Jackson blushed. "I couldn't let anything happen to my bride-to-be."

Marianne looked at Jackson and Allison. "I think I'll head up to bed for a rest. Bella, would you give me a hand so we can leave these two lovebirds alone?" asked Marianne. "They have a wedding to plan."

Bella smiled and added, "That, they do."

2020

Chapter 49

Three Years Later

Allison reached out for Jackson's large body beside her in the king-sized bed, only to find him missing. She loved him so much. Ever since he'd retired and they had married, the past three years had been the best of her life. Her marriage brought her a sense of completeness, as did her more settled boys. It was a happy home with a loving husband and her handsome, playful boys who loved her, often visiting with their sweethearts. Danny had come out, and Allison was proud to talk about her gay son. His brothers in more macho careers took his news in stride, loving him too much to push him away because he was in love with another man.

Allison heard Jackson approaching, his cell phone in hand. He leaned down and kissed her on the forehead. "It's for you."

"Is it time?"

He nodded, and Allison's heart dropped. She'd been expecting the call, although she wished away the reason for it. She listened to the caller and then said, "Yes, I'm on my way."

Devastated, Allison called Bella.

♥ ♥ ♥

Bella knew as soon as she heard her phone ring … it was time. She hurried to make the necessary arrangements, hating the reason for them.

She was grateful that she'd had time to finish up at Doctors Without Borders and get resettled into her home in California. She wasn't sure how long California would be her home since Cam had fallen in love with Allison's son Erik, a fireman and part-time first responder driving an ambulance throughout Boston during the covid pandemic. He made Cam laugh, and Bella was grateful to Erik for that alone after Cam's rough start in life. They were happy together, and that was all that mattered to Bella.

Perhaps that was what she needed as well. To learn to laugh again and spend time with Allison's family, eradicating the unhappiness of living in today's world where so much was needed to right the world in their moral responsibilities to each other. Bella sighed. If her grandmother were alive, she'd be so disheartened with the events of today and its lack of civility.

♥ ♥ ♥

Because of a delay with Allison's flight, she and Bella arrived at the airport around the same time. William was there waiting for them with a sadness that came from knowing that these would be Marianne's last days.

Once at Marianne's house, a nurse ushered them upstairs to the master bedroom of the house she had bought several years ago to be closer to her granddaughter. Her bedroom was bright, and the windows were open, letting in the mild air. As always, Marianne's talent for decorating stood out, making anyone who visited feel ensconced in comfort and beauty.

Andrew met them at the doorway of his mother's room, and when he saw them, he smiled with pleasure. "We're so glad you came."

Marianne's granddaughter stepped from behind her father and smiled at them. "Hi, Auntie Allison and Auntie Bella!"

"Hi, Sweetheart," Allison responded, hugging her and passing her onto Bella.

"You've grown so much since I saw you last, Sweetie!" exclaimed Bella.

"I know," she giggled.

"We're going now, so you three ladies have some privacy without "little big ears" here," he chuckled.

"Oh, Dad," moaned Isabella.

"We'll come back later," he promised.

Allison passed by Andrew, and her breath drew in with surprise at seeing Marianne resting back regally amid the pillows against her headboard. She was stunningly beautiful in her fragility and translucent skin. When Marianne saw her and Bella, her smile widened, and her eyes shone with love for them. Cuddled by her side, Sophie, her latest poodle dog, watched with interest.

"So glad you could make the farewell party," Marianne joked, immediately setting the stage for her final days.

On the many occasions that Sarah went upstairs to check on the girls, she could hear them laughing. Sometimes, she stood outside the door and chuckled along with them as they talked about what it was like to have reached the age of being invisible.

"There has to be more in life than wondering if you're going to reach the bathroom in time," laughed Allison. "Or wondering why you're standing in front of the refrigerator trying to remember what you wanted!"

The girls laughed. "What's the most stupid thing you've ever done?" Marianne asked them.

"You mean besides allowing Benjamin to stay with me while he pursued his old girlfriend?" asked Bella.

The girls howled at her exasperation.

And it went on and on like that with the stories they shared. The days slipped by. Often, Sarah would peek inside to find the three women spread across Marianne's king-sized bed napping with her, causing Sarah to tear up and cry over their devotion to each other.

They all knew the final day had arrived, and it would be Marianne's last one. Allison and Bella stood aside as they ushered in the family members and a few friends to say their final goodbyes. Jeremy had arrived sobbing and sat in the corner inconsolable. He was making so much noise that Bella asked him if he wanted to speak with Marianne.

At first, he refused. Then he rose and bent over Marianne. "You were the best thing in my life, Marianne. I still love you."

"Ditto," she whispered.

At Marianne's urging, the room was cleared of everyone but the three of them. Allison gripped one hand and Bella the other as the time came for her to leave. "I love you, dear sisters. Thank you for being here," she struggled to say.

One second she was there; then she wasn't, her spirit rising with a part of her soul left behind in the hearts of her two best friends—the women she'd met in the Waiting Room.

After the funeral, Allison and Bella left Atlanta and headed to Boston, where Erik and Cam would meet them at the airport. With Marianne no longer a part of their threesome, the two were aware of their surviving a mutual loss and finding solace in each other. Both were grateful for the opportunity to have become friends so long ago.

A sudden flash of understanding passed between them. Isn't that what life was all about? That continuous seeking to rediscover each other once again as the soul mates they once were? Without thought, Allison and Bella reached for each other's hand and held on tight.

J.S. PECK

Joan was reared in a family of readers in small-town Elmira, New York. Each Sunday afternoon was a special time where each member of her family was able to relax with a good book. She was raised to be opened-minded, and discussion about her beliefs was encouraged. Joan came to the understanding that we are all connected energetically and can communicate with others who have passed on. Drawn to her spiritual and supernatural beliefs, Joan brings that idea into all of her writings and expresses in her work her interest to shatter the power of addiction and human trafficking.

Joan is an editor and author of short stories, spiritual books, and has a mystery book series called The Death Card Series. Her book, *Prime Threat – Shattering the Power of Addiction,* has helped many who are looking to understand addiction in a whole new way. She is also a contributing writer for *Choices* magazine and serves as the Editor in Chief for *Chic Compass* magazine, produced in Las Vegas and available world-wide.

"I hope you enjoyed reading this book. If so, and you feel inspired, please help other readers discover it by leaving your honest review. Reviews are what helps an author to succeed. Thank you for your kindness."

ACKNOWLEDGMENTS

Many thanks to all those in my family, others, and my beautiful readers who have supported me on my journey of writing mysteries and my other books. It's heartwarming to have your encouragement.

I was blessed when I contacted Kelly Martin to be my book cover designer. Thank you, Kelly, for your creativity and artistic talents. I love your work and you.

Thank you, Jake Naylor, for designing my website, being my layout person, and so much more. You're a marvel, and you're the best. I could never have done this without you. I appreciate and love you.

BOOKS BY J.S. PECK

The Death Card Series
- Book 1: *Death on the Strip*
- Book 2: *Death at the Lake*
- Book 3: *Death Returns*
- Book 4: *Death Waits*
- Book 5: *Death on the Run*
- Book 6: *Death Comes Calling*

- *Angels Out of the Dark*
- *The Waiting Room*
- *Santa Baby* … Out in 2022

BOOKS BY JOAN S. PECK

- *The Seven Major Chakras – Keeping it Simple*
- *A Simple Approach to Living a Successful Life*
- *What You Need to Know to Live a Spiritual Life*
- *Prime Threat – Shattering the Power of Addiction*

Made in the USA
Columbia, SC
21 June 2022